# FREE NINA
## THE COLLEGE YEARS

Edward "EJ" Mulraine

*Free Nina: The College Years*

Copyright © 2022 by Edward Mulraine. All rights reserved.

---

No part of this publication may be reproduced, stored in a retrieval system or transmitted in any way by any means, electronic, mechanical, photocopy, recording or otherwise without the prior permission of the author except as provided by USA copyright law.

# TABLE OF CONTENTS

Chapter One . . . . . . . . . . . . . . . . . . . . . . . . . . . . . . . . . 1

Chapter Two . . . . . . . . . . . . . . . . . . . . . . . . . . . . . . . . . 2

Chapter Three . . . . . . . . . . . . . . . . . . . . . . . . . . . . . . . 11

Chapter Four . . . . . . . . . . . . . . . . . . . . . . . . . . . . . . . . 17

Chapter Five . . . . . . . . . . . . . . . . . . . . . . . . . . . . . . . . . 21

Chapter Six . . . . . . . . . . . . . . . . . . . . . . . . . . . . . . . . . . 31

Chapter Seven . . . . . . . . . . . . . . . . . . . . . . . . . . . . . . . 40

Chapter Eight . . . . . . . . . . . . . . . . . . . . . . . . . . . . . . . . 53

Chapter Nine . . . . . . . . . . . . . . . . . . . . . . . . . . . . . . . . 56

Chapter Ten . . . . . . . . . . . . . . . . . . . . . . . . . . . . . . . . . 65

Chapter Eleven . . . . . . . . . . . . . . . . . . . . . . . . . . . . . . . 74

Chapter Twelve . . . . . . . . . . . . . . . . . . . . . . . . . . . . . . . 87

Chapter Thirteen . . . . . . . . . . . . . . . . . . . . . . . . . . . . . 95

Chapter Fourteen . . . . . . . . . . . . . . . . . . . . . . . . . . . 105

Chapter Fifteen . . . . . . . . . . . . . . . . . . . . . . . . . . . . . . . . . . .107

Chapter Sixteen. . . . . . . . . . . . . . . . . . . . . . . . . . . . . . . . . . .113

Chapter Seventeen . . . . . . . . . . . . . . . . . . . . . . . . . . . . . . . .133

Chapter Eighteen . . . . . . . . . . . . . . . . . . . . . . . . . . . . . . . . .140

Chapter Nineteen . . . . . . . . . . . . . . . . . . . . . . . . . . . . . . . . .145

Chapter Twenty. . . . . . . . . . . . . . . . . . . . . . . . . . . . . . . . . . .154

Chapter Twenty-One . . . . . . . . . . . . . . . . . . . . . . . . . . . . . .158

Chapter Twenty-Two. . . . . . . . . . . . . . . . . . . . . . . . . . . . . . .172

Chapter Twenty-Three . . . . . . . . . . . . . . . . . . . . . . . . . . . . .175

Chapter Twenty-Four . . . . . . . . . . . . . . . . . . . . . . . . . . . . . .189

# CHAPTER ONE

Everything born in man and woman is found in the soul. It must then be nurtured for their true character to emerge. At the end of life, each man and woman seek comfort and peace of the soul, but first, each must experience all the drama of life to make that peace possible. Some seek comfort in others because of their nature, others because of loss, and others because it seeks them.

Christopher Lee Raine was a man-child, precious and fearless, full of energy and imagination, whose craving for presence was born of absence and emptiness. At his young age, sorrow engulfed him through the loss of his father, who embodied to the child masculinity and courage. His hero provided protection and gave him a sense of being and belonging and a purpose to fulfill for others. Although his hero could no longer be seen, he could be found, heard in the inner places of the conscious that gave guidance and direction but, most of all, balance against inner demons and external foes.

# CHAPTER TWO

June 1986

Chris had always been a restless kid, and this June day was no exception. The boundless energy that animated him was caused by his cousin's promise to take him for a ride in his brand-new car. Chris had awoken already in a frenzy of excitement at the prospect. He rolled out of bed, the covers trailing behind him as if he were superman with his cape cascading from his shoulders. He bounded to the window to check the view outside, searching first up and then down the street. Making sure his cousin hadn't arrived while he slept. Frantic, he worried. *"What if I've missed him?"* The thought was too painful to entertain.

Chris ran to the bathroom, barely brushing his teeth and splashing water on his face, before hurrying back to jump into the matching sweatpants and jacket he had laid out the night before in anticipation of his big day. He opened his closet and perused the selection of sneakers, finally pulling out a pair of

Adidas emblazoned with black stripes to match the color of his sweat suit. Fully adorned, he looked in the mirror, added a New York Knicks cap, and proclaimed to himself, "I'm the Man!"

He bolted downstairs to find his mom standing in the kitchen with an empty milk bottle in her hand. In cool, measured tones that did nothing to disguise her displeasure, she commanded, "Chris, come here."

He looked anxiously once more towards the window before quickly making his way towards where his mother stood in front of the open refrigerator door, frowning into the cold light. As he skidded to a halt half a foot away, she asked, "What happened to all the milk?"

"I dunno."

"*I dunno.*" She mimicked him. "You're almost fifteen. I'm sure you can talk better than that."

"Did you guzzle it all last night? It had to be you. I haven't seen your cousin in three days."

Chris shrugged, bobbing impatiently from foot to foot. *Gotta get back to the window. Don't miss him.*

"I was planning on using it for biscuits." Her tone made it clear that she would not overlook his behavior. There was no point in making excuses, so Chris stood silently, waiting for her to name his punishment. Even so, he was stunned by her pronouncement. "Now, you're going to have to run down to the corner store and buy me a gallon! Right away!" Implacable yet calm, her voice seemed to echo in the stillness.

"I can't, Mom—"

"Don't fuss at me, boy. I'm in no mood. Goodbye." She slammed the refrigerator door.

He could see his dream of the perfect day slipping away. "Later, okay?" he whined. "Damon and me, we was going—"

"Damon," she huffed. "I love him, but that boy is nothing but trouble." She turned away; the empty bottle set accusingly on the countertop. Her hands were busy digging through her purse as she ignored every excuse he tried. Chris couldn't give in; he continued to fire objections at her. "We made this plan last week, and he's driving here specifically to take me out. I haven't driven in the new car yet, and you promised I could go with him today."

In response, she held out two-dollar bills. "Here. That should be more than enough. You're getting off easy. I should make you pay for it since you drank it. Now get your butt down to the store."

Chris sighed and shook his head. When she got like this, there was no arguing with her. But he couldn't give up. This was his day to hang out with his cousin, the coolest, slickest dude there was. He couldn't pass up a day with him over a carton of milk.

Suddenly the solution hit him. "Fine, Mom, Damon can drive me to the store as soon as he gets here." Chris dared to hope as his mother cocked her head, thinking about his plan.

"We'll pick up the milk and be back here so fast it'll still be ice cold. All the better for biscuit makin', right?"

He didn't know if the idea appealed to her or if he'd just worn her down. She finally waved him away, and he ran out of the kitchen. He took being dismissed without further instruction to mean she was cool with the plan.

Chris hadn't even reached the front window when he heard: "Hey yo, C! Come on, get in da car!"

Damon had arrived in style. He pulled up in his new black 1986 Buick Regal Coupe. The car glinted like a black diamond. It was glistening, like he had just come from the car wash. Tinted windows sparkled. Chrome gleamed from the Armor All.

Chris snagged the Game Boy Damon had given him for his birthday and ran out to the car. Damon wore his signature attire: a black Kangol hat, black hoodie, Gazelle glasses, and a fat gold chain around his neck.

Chris grinned as he jumped into the passenger seat of the two-door coupe. "Where we goin'?"

"You'll see." Damon winked.

Chris looked out the side window. His mom stood on the stoop, her hands on her hips. She wasn't smiling. Damon waved at her, but she just looked at him unhappily, then pointed her finger and said, "Watch it out there." Then she walked back into the house.

"First, we gotta do something," Chris whispered, hoping Damon wouldn't get upset. "I promised Mom we'd stop at the store for milk."

"Seriously, man?"

Chris nodded his head solemnly. "She'll kill me if we don't."

"All right then. Milk." He rolled his eyes, but then he nodded. "Okay, cool. I know where we can get it. Let's drive to the old hood. You know where we all used to live in the South Bronx?" Damon loved to drive; the farther, the better. Up the street wasn't good enough for him.

"Okay, let's go, but let's be careful like mom said." Damon just looked at Chris and sped off.

As they drove across town, music blasted through the speakers in the trunk of Damon's car. The whole neighborhood could hear them. Older people looked annoyed as they drove loudly by, but younger people danced along to the music when they stopped at a red light. Chris watched for them as they turned each corner, seeing how the music seemed to turn every street they drove down into a block party.

At one light, a couple of crackheads ran toward the car, calling Damon's name. He jammed his foot down on the accelerator when he saw them coming and quickly left them behind. He drove Chris back to and through their old neighborhood, where crack was heavy and abandoned buildings plentiful. At night, this would be a dark and dangerous haven of prostitutes and drug dealers who emerged like rats from the tenements and took over the streets. During the day, though, with the sun shining down, even on the broken bricks of abandoned buildings, it just felt to Chris like home, the 'old hood' when they both were small.

Damon enjoyed the attention as people on the street recognized him and waved. Chris was proud, enjoying the approval of their wheels. Damon drove with his right hand on the steering wheel and his left arm hanging out the car window. "Criminal Minded" by KRS-One played on his tape deck as they bobbed their heads to the beat and sang along with the lyrics.

They stopped in front of the bodega just down the street from Chris's old apartment building. Damon turned off the engine and jumped out of the car. The music stopped.

Chris groaned. "Damn, why you turn off my joint?"

"Stay here. I'll be right back with the milk." He held out his hand, and Chris laid two dollars in his upturned palm.

As Damon bounced off, Chris grumbled beneath his breath but then turned to his Game Boy. It had been one of the great gifts that Damon always seemed to get Chris, expensive stuff he somehow managed to get whenever Chris requested it.

A few minutes later, Damon came out of the store. Chris glanced up and saw Damon breezin' along, a jug of milk in one hand, a big grin on his face as he gazed with pride at his car. Chris looked back down at his game.

Suddenly gunshots cracked the air from somewhere nearby.

Chris dropped the Game Boy and ducked instinctively. He waited a couple of seconds after the shooting stopped, then slowly stuck his head up and looked out the window.

When he looked up, Damon was lying on the ground, on his back. He wasn't moving. Chris barely registered the figures running away down the street as he jumped out of the car and rushed to Damon's body.

"Damon!" He yelled, dropping onto the ground beside his cousin. The plastic jug had split open when it fell—milk mixed with blood pooled on the ground by his body. Chris couldn't tell where the blood was coming from, but his mouth gaped open, and he could see it was full of liquid. His hat had fallen off, the gold chain gone. Chris sensed people shouting and moving around him, but he couldn't look away from Damon. Not even for a second. He gently removed his glasses and peered into Damon's still face. *Don't die,* he thought. *Please, please...please don't die.* Chris cradled his cousin's head in his lap.

"Somebody, call the ambulance!" He shouted, his voice cracking. "Somebody, please call the police!"

A small crowd had gathered around them. The store owner came out, then ran back inside the bodega Damon had exited just moments before.

Damon stared up at Chris. Suddenly his lips moved as if he was struggling to speak around the blood. He choked on it.

"I'm a'ight," he wheezed. "Them suckers is bad shots. Wait till I get them bastards."

"Shut up, just...just hang on." Chris scrambled for something to use to stem the blood. His hat was the only thing in reach. He pushed the hat to Damon's chest, where he thought he saw blood oozing out, and in seconds the hat was soaked. There was just so much of it. He couldn't stop the flow.

Damon's eyes kept sliding closed. Chris's tears fell onto his face; his voice rose to an anguished scream. An eternity later, he finally heard the sirens of an approaching ambulance. Damon clutched Chris's hand hard, so hard it hurt.

Chris smiled reassuringly; he didn't know what to say. He remembered a scene from a TV cop show. "They're almost here. They'll take care of you."

"I'm good," Damon said, spitting up more blood. "Yo, C, don't worry 'bout me. I'm good."

Medics swarmed around them. Someone pulled Chris's hand out of Damon's grip.

"We need to take over from here, kid," one of the EMTs said while easing Chris away from his cousin. They moved Damon onto a stretcher.

"I need to go with him. To the hospital!" Chris shouted, gasping for breath between sobs. Chris staggered across the pavement toward the ambulance, following the gurney.

But before he could climb into the ambulance, one of the police officers grabbed him by the back of his shirt and threw him down to the ground, pinning him with his arms immobilized, like a criminal. He kicked and screamed, "That's my cousin, man. They shot him! Why the hell you holding *me* down? Let me go, assholes!"

Chris saw the EMTs working frantically through the open ambulance doors on Damon. Then an attendant slammed the doors closed, and the vehicle was gone.

"No-o-o!" Chris wailed as the ambulance siren receded.

The cops were still holding him down, his cheek grinding into the pavement, his arms twisted painfully behind his back. And although he couldn't see it—he felt the blood drying on his skin, seeping into his clothes—Damon's blood.

The next day, Chris woke up in the hospital with the smell of blood lingering in his nose and the sight of his cousin's terrified face still clear in his mind's eye. The blood had not only stained his clothes and nose but had gotten into his young soul.

# CHAPTER THREE

### April 1992

It takes time for a person to overcome grief; when not ignited, trauma can be subdued and hidden if not controlled. Chris had finally made it from the nights of days to the days of nights. The blood and terror that had seeped into his soul had been calmed, and he was not haunted by day or night by his past but happy and content in his new environment. He had gone from the hoods of violence to the woods of college. His pure energy and restless spirit had found a refuge when he shifted from a community filled with intra-racial crime to a college campus, although one tainted with inter-racial injustice.

As men have always, he sought comfort for his troubled soul in a good woman's arms.

"Come on, Nina, just trust me," Chris coaxed.

"No, Chris, we promised to wait," Nina responded softly as Chris continued to kiss her passionately on the twin-size bed in his dorm room. Despite her protests, she seemed as caught up in the sensual moment as he was.

"I know," he sighed as he kissed her lips and caressed her butt through her clothes, "and we *have* waited, two and a half years babe, we kept our promise. What are we waiting for?"

Nina made a sound of frustration, pushed Chris off her, and jumped out of bed. He landed on the floor.

Putting on her jacket, she headed towards the door. "You think you're slick, but I'm serious," she said over her shoulder. "Come on, I have to change for class, and you have that final today. I hope you're ready. It could mean the difference between your graduating with honors or not."

"Yeah, I'm ready," Chris said despondently as he pushed himself up from the floor, adjusting his pants to obscure his erection.

Chris walked Nina across campus to her dorm room the way he always did. It was seven in the morning, foggy but warm. Nina lived across the manicured green lawn, also known as the quad. To Chris, it felt like they walked down the red carpet every time they crossed it.

As they walked, Chris reminisced about the first time they met. Nina had been coming toward him across the quad. Her braids pulled back in a ponytail that draped over her neck and shoulders. Her caramel skin was flawless, her wide smile endless, and her graceful body peerless. As she came closer, he could see her eyes, obsidian jewels so dark they glowed. She tried to pass him, but Chris held out his hand with all the confidence he had ever possessed and introduced himself. It worked. She stopped and considered him.

She stood about 5'5, her chin on a level with his shoulder. He could imagine how she'd feel, her head tucked into his neck, the perfect fit. Her voice, when she spoke, was mellow and her handshake firm. Nina had been a second-semester freshman, and Chris a second-semester sophomore. He played it cool, inviting her to a poetry reading that the Black Student Union was having for Black History Month. She came that night in her African dashiki and recited "Ain't I a Woman?" by Sojourner Truth. Her reading shook him; her voice was soft yet strong, like a quiet storm. He wasn't the only one she had touched; some in the audience cried. Everyone laughed at the right moments. When she finished the reading, she received thunderous applause.

Someone from the Black Student Union asked Chris who she was, and he replied firmly:

"My girl."

Since that first meeting, Chris and Nina had been inseparable. She had captured both his senses and his mind and was equally captivated by him and his beliefs. They worked together, not only as a couple but in every way. They had the same views and were dedicated students determined to wring every ounce they could out of the college and give something back.

The other students admired them and what they did together, often calling them the Martin and Coretta Scott King of campus activism. They often held hands as they walked through the campus. Chris, overprotective of Nina, was 5'11 with a slim, muscular build. He was a handsome young man with dark skin, chiseled cheekbones, and low-cut hair with perfect edges. He had developed the art of communicating and the consciousness for Black people that his father had instilled in him, and he conveyed it with the attitude and uncompromising bluntness his mother had nurtured in him. Both Chris and Nina were from The Bronx but didn't know each other until they met on campus.

Nina supported Chris's aspirations and goals, particularly his ambition to achieve. As they walked, they often engaged in dialogue about the issues facing Black people.

"I hope you mentioned Black women and the injustices of the system." They had been talking about the paper Chris had been working on for one of his classes. As always, Nina was quick to cut to the heart of the matter. "You men often forget about women's suffering, but the system affects us too, sometimes even worse. Take slavery for example." Nina stopped and looked up at Chris as if he were the enemy. "Women had to suffer double the pain just by virtue of being female. Black and White men both were guilty of mistreating Black women."

"Of course," Chris assured her. Reaching for Nina, he spun her around and kissed her in the middle of the lawn, partially concealed by a light morning fog covering the green expanse.

"Oh, Chris, stop. Concentrate on your work. Not working on me." Nina smiled as she tried to loosen his grip on her waist.

In less than five minutes, they arrived at Nina's dorm door. She turned to him. "How do you think you'll do today in the debate?"

"You know I'll take that White boy down." Chris smiled and brushed her cheek with his knuckles, studying her lovely face rather than listening to her words. Letting his hand fall, he said more seriously, "I've been preparing for this moment. I'm ready."

Nina sighed, relaxing. "I know you'll do well," She nodded as if reminding herself as much as him. "You're the greatest when it comes to these things. Just don't get big-headed. You know you can get a little crazy. Don't start repeating yourself." Nina kissed Chris, and they hugged for a moment before she opened the door and ran upstairs to her room.

"Yeah, I got this," Chris chuckled and shouted after her as she ran up the stairs. "And don't worry. The only person I'm crazy about is you!" Nina smiled as she entered her room.

Chris ran across the quad back to his room to prepare for class. Since he'd been fooling around with Nina, he hadn't finished preparing the last part of his argument for the debate. Nina was right. Chris needed to add more points concerning the criminal justice system's impact on Black women. This debate was important because it would determine his final grade, and he wanted to ace it.

Chris did a little more research and wrote some more. When he looked up, it was three minutes after nine. "Damn!" The class started at nine. He was officially late.

Throwing on his jacket, he raced across the lawn.

# CHAPTER FOUR

"Hey, Nina, how are you?" Tracy was sitting at her desk as Nina walked in. They had been roommates since freshman year and were as close as sisters.

Nina stepped into her room. It was much bigger than Chris's bedroom—two beds, two desks, and a closet she and her roommate shared.

"Hey, Tracy. What you doing?" Nina took off her jacket and made her way over to her bed. She'd chosen to use Pan-African flag colors in the black, red, and green quilt she'd made, with pillows to match. Over her bed hung a picture of Angela Davis, a radical Black feminist of the 1960s.

"Nothing. Just a little work for class. I stayed out a little late last night with Joey." Tracy looked up from the textbook she had been reading and smiled. Her straight blond hair fell across her face, and she brushed it away to focus her blue eyes on Nina.

"Joey, who?" Nina inquired as she sat on her bed, taking off her shoes.

"Come on, Nina, you know Jooooey."

"I thought you were going out with Paul or Peter. One of them guys."

"Really, Nina. Paul is old news."

"Well, excuse me for not keeping up with current events." They both laughed.

"Enough about me." Tracy looked up at Nina with a smirk, tapping a pencil to the corner of her mouth. "So, did you and Chris finally get it in last night?"

"Tracy, you know I'm not going there," Nina responded, but she couldn't help blushing. Nina fell back onto her bed as if it were a pool of cool water. "Although…I must admit, it gets harder and harder each time we're together."

"Oh, do you mean *he* gets harder and harder each time you're together." Tracy teased.

Nina turned over to lay on her stomach. She hugged her pillow as if it were Chris himself.

"Yeah, and it feels so-o-o-o good." Nina blushed even more at her guilty pleasure. "We keep getting closer and closer. But then I stop, even though I want to keep going."

"Well, if you get wet and he gets hard, that's a perfect combination. Just do it. I mean, girlfriend, it's been like ten years."

"No, Tracy!" Nina shot back as she lifted herself up and threw a pillow at her roommate. "It's only been two-and-a-half years. And I am ready. I just want to be sure."

"Well, girlfriend. If you're not sure by now, when will you be?" Tracy gave Nina a long, solemn look. "Two-and-a-half years is a long time to make a man wait. I know you're a virgin and all, but once you do it, you will keep wanting it. Believe me." Tracy gave her a mischievous wink.

Nina rolled her eyes. "I know you're the expert, with your vast experience with men. But this virgin must be super sure because I know how men change after getting it. And I'm not going to let no one run up in me and then treat me like dirt. If they love you, they will wait."

Nina jumped up from her bed and went to the closet.

"Do you like this shirt, Tracy."

"Yeah, it's nice, but don't try to change the subject."

Nina ignored her. She put the shirt on her bed and started looking for a pair of pants to go with it.

"I doubt if Chris is going to change," Tracy said. "He's been with you for two-plus years. Waiting, just like you wanted."

Nina avoided her roommate's gaze and looked at Tracy's bed, which was a mess. The pink sheets and pillows had slid halfway off, and the white blanket was crumpled on the floor as if more than one person had slept in it.

"Are you cleaning up your side of the room today?" Nina said, trying to deflect the conversation away from the topic.

Tracy was unstoppable. "I'm serious. Most guys who are fake leave in two days or less. Chris has proven he loves you. He may not like me, but he loves you. The thing is, and take it from an expert on the male species, if you don't give him some, he may not leave you, but he will find some other ass to take care of his physical needs, especially since he's graduating this year."

Nina pretended not to hear as she surveyed a pair of pants she'd pulled from the closet, but she wondered, *Could Tracy be right about Chris?*

Just then, there was a loud knock at the door. Nina quickly crossed the room to open it. Two of Chris's homeys stood in the hall. "Barry, DJ, what's up?"

"Everything! Where's Chris?" Barry stepped halfway into the room and looked around, ignoring Tracy.

"He's in class. Why? What's going on. You banging like the police is after you."

"No, it's more serious than that. We just got a tip, and we need you and Chris to come and bust some shit up with us."

"Come on, we'll tell you on the way," DJ said as Nina slipped on her shoes.

"Can I come, too?" Tracy called out softly.

"Hell no!" Barry and DJ yelled at the same time.

"Come on, let's go." Barry grabbed Nina by the hand. She dropped the pants she was still holding and trotted along behind them.

# CHAPTER FIVE

Outside, it was a lovely day. The sun had burnt through the clouds and the morning air was balmy. The stage was being set up for Quad Jam, which would take place in three days.

Every year, the school threw a huge concert on the lawn right before May graduation. Chris's class, the class of '92, was graduating this year. Manhattanville College had a small yet beautiful campus with about twenty-five hundred students —75% White, 12% Black, 7% Hispanic, 6% Asian, and 'other.' Located in wealthy Westchester County, New York. The college was approximately thirty-five minutes from New York City by car, which was why Chris had chosen it after high school. He needed to be away from home but not too far away. If something happened, he could get back home in an hour or less.

The campus was a total departure from the neighborhood where Chris had grown up in The Bronx. Trees and a thick green lawn covered the campus. The gated walls made him feel like he was living in a luxury housing complex. The majority White population and other ethnic groups created a completely exotic atmosphere; he felt as if half an hour from home, he'd found a foreign country. It seemed like the sun always shone, even in the winter. The lily-white school was proud of its academics and alumni, which included a Kennedy.

Quad Jam attracted media coverage, mainly because of the famous bands booked to perform. The venue was the bright green, oval-shaped lawn that stretched a quarter-mile through the middle of the campus, separating the dorms on one side from the academic buildings and library on the other. At the top of the lawn was a towering Brandywine-stone castle that imbued the school with prestige and distinction. It was called Reid Castle, named after the former estate of Whitelaw Reid, owner of *The New York Tribune*.

The castle impressed Chris because it reminded him of Disney World, which he had dreamed of visiting since he was a kid. When he walked into the castle, it was just as opulent as the outside suggested—dark wood walls, stone staircases, marble floors, and numerous rooms. These days, it is used for faculty and administrative offices and grand fundraising events for some of the rich folks in town. It was a complete contrast to the shattered tenement buildings in The Bronx.

It took Chris less than three minutes to run to class. When he got there, the student he was to debate was already holding forth about the Rockefeller Drug Laws, just as he had expected. The debate topic was the draconian and cruel laws that Governor Nelson Rockefeller had implemented in 1973, which, in the end, negatively affected primarily African Americans in urban communities. Today, nineteen years after the laws passage, they were still controversial. Unsurprisingly, since they imposed a mandatory minimum sentence of fifteen years on people arrested in possession of four ounces of an illegal drug or for selling two ounces of heroin, cocaine, or crack. The user was sentenced with the same harshness as the seller, effectively taking away sentencing discretion from judges. As a result, plea bargaining was limited.

All in all, these laws produced prison overcrowding and broke up families, particularly families of color. Chris's final paper delved into their unfairness to minority communities, and he was more than ready to debate his position.

About 20 students filled the small conference room. Heads turned briefly to stare at Chris as he rushed in, then turned back to the student presenting the Pro side of the debate. Professor Hines, seated at his desk between the two podiums, observed Chris with a mixture of disapproval and appreciation. He had been Chris's advisor, mentor, and professor for all four college years. He knew Chris would provide an alternative perspective to the conservative rationale. Chris was outspoken on racial and political matters and often debated furiously with some of the college's conservative students—White *and* Black. While the school was considered liberal, it was attended by several politically and fiscally conservative thinkers who would not hesitate to give their traditional – and at times racist – opinions on matters.

Dr. Hines was a very casual dresser; a button-down shirt under a sweater and a pair of khaki pants were his signature attire. His long, salt-and-pepper hair would have made him look like a hippie if it hadn't been for the glasses that hung down his nose. A former student radical but now calm in his demeanor and sophisticated in his approach to teaching, not allowing too much of his perspective to dominate the students' discussions. Chris thought his Jewish background gave him empathy for the oppressed. A definite liberal, Professor Hines spoke out in his books and articles against conservative political policies.

Thanks to his resume, Professor Hines was a regular on political talk shows and a sought-after political advisor for elected officials. He enjoyed egging on his students, encouraging them to argue their perspectives, and challenging their knowledge. He began each class with a discussion on the most current events, usually from *The New York Times*. He made the students want to read and stay informed about national politics and social issues because he made clear the connection between politics and social justice.

Thomas, the student Chris was to debate, stood to the right of Professor Hines. As Chris approached the front of the classroom, Thomas tore into the issue with an insult that infuriated Chris.

"Since Black people commit the most crimes in their neighborhoods, the laws were implemented to protect Black people from Black drug dealers. When Rockefeller fought for the laws, he sought the advice of Black preachers, who also supported the laws. Back then, it was about heroin; today it's about crack, which is killing their community. An atrocity they just allow to happen; the same way in which they allow abortion clinics into their neighborhoods to kill their children. Why is it that most abortion clinics are in the Black community?" The silence stretched as if he were encouraging his audience to fill in the blanks. He looked at Chris with an arrogant smirk on his face.

Chris met his challenging gaze but held back from responding until it was his time to speak, as per the rules of the debate.

"But the discussion today is about drugs," he continued. "These laws were created to save the lives of African Americans and even White Americans from criminals in their neighborhoods—that's a good thing."

Thomas Mahone, also known as Tommy, was a stout Irish kid from Buffalo, New York. At 5'7, the redhead was more into books than girls. He dressed in casual beige suits and bow ties like a scholar. He and a few of his comrades made it their business to speak out on conservative matters. He was proud to represent the minority of students at the college who were conservative.

To Chris, he and his crew were nothing but racists. They were anti-Black, anti-poor, anti-gay, anti-integration, and anti-immigration. The conservative students were always defending America and every atrocity committed on her soil, including segregation, housing discrimination, police shootings of African Americans, and the broken criminal justice system.

Tommy had been in many of Chris's classes since freshman year, and they had gotten to know each other both in class and on campus. They never agreed on anything except to disagree on everything. He hung with his crew, which included many in the Student Government, and Chris hung with his, which included most of the Black Student Union.

Professor Hines beckoned Chris forward and briefly interrupted Tommy to greet his opponent. "Chris, nice of you to join us."

Chris quickly apologized for his lateness and made his way to the podium on the left, giving Tommy a dirty look as he passed by him. While he made his way, Professor Hines repeated the rules of the debate. Each person had five minutes to present, two minutes to rebut the opponent's argument, and two more minutes to wrap up. Since Tommy was on time, he had been given the opening five minutes, then Chris would have his turn.

As soon as Tommy finished his impassioned speech, Chris immediately jumped in without needing to refer to his notes. He had memorized his opening argument. "I believe the Rockefeller Drug Laws were originally implemented to curb drug use." Chris was calm in his demeanor as he stared directly at Tommy. "But the final implementation was unfair and extreme. The laws hurt the vulnerable and took away the judges' discretion to determine whether the offender deserved the minimum sentence required by the law. The law took power away from judges to be lenient with minors and first-time offenders.

The mandatory minimum is a death sentence even for first-time offenders accused of handling and using drugs. It's an immoral law because it has no consideration or feelings for those who are addicts due to extenuating circumstances. Both Republicans and Democrats denounced the law as extreme, and only after many compromises did it pass in the first place — with mostly Republican support."

Tommy looked at Chris as if he were going to jump in before Chris's five minutes were up, but luckily, he managed to restrain himself.

"Although you mention preachers supporting the measure, Tommy," Chris shot him a venomous look, "the law has been consistently denounced, and several of its provisions overturned because of Black preachers and legislators in Albany acknowledging the negative effects it has had on Black communities, families, and the economy. They recognized the injustice and inhumanity of the law. Just look at the prison population and its burgeoning costs because of the Rockefeller laws. The prison population soared because of an influx of minors, Black men, Black women, and first-time offenders, most of whom are nonviolent offenders. This has cost the state a considerable amount of money to house and build prisons constantly. Rehabilitating addicts and putting first-time offenders and minors on probation would have been much less costly."

At the expression on Tommy's face, Chris shook his head in disgust, "I would think that you—being a fiscal conservative—would understand the extreme cost of overcrowded prisons and how that money can go to better use."

The bell rang for Tommy's two-minute rebuttal.

Irate, Tommy slashed a hand through the air. "No!" He shot back, "First of all, crime is down because of the laws. Fewer drug dealers and criminals are on the street, and more are behind bars where they belong."

"What good are they if crime is down and the prison population is up? All it means is that we've put every Black person in jail!" Chris shot back out of turn. Professor Hines looked at Chris warningly. He quickly apologized and Tommy continued.

"America is so good to the guilty that it affords them a legal aid attorney if they want to fight the charges," Tommy stated arrogantly. The bell rang!

"Ask people who have been through the *injustice* system how effective their legal aid lawyer was! Ask them if they got off. You're a smart guy, Tommy. Look at the statistics for people who have legal aid lawyers and people who hire private attorneys and see if they're getting fair and effective representation. It's not because legal aid lawyers are incompetent; it's because they're overburdened with drug cases, and they'd rather their clients cop a deal." The bell rang.

Tommy's face was bright red, and his mouth was a tight, angry line. He knew he was losing the fight but wouldn't acknowledge the truth.

"The law has reduced the number of drug dealers *and* users in the urban communities. *That* should be our measuring tool." The bell rang.

"No!" Chris snapped, "Our measuring tool should be whether the law is being implemented fairly, whether the law is working to rehabilitate people back into society, and whether the law has a conscience that takes cases on a personal basis rather than treating every offender the same way." The bell rang!

Just as Tommy was about to continue, Professor Hines spoke up. "Thank you, thank you, you two!" The professor interrupted loudly, ending the debate. The class stood and erupted in applause. Chris took a bow, and Tommy stood back, defeated. Professor Hines stood encouraging Chris and Tommy to shake each other's hands, which they did with reluctance.

Professor Hines asked if there were any questions. Chris looked around for Tommy's conservative friends to defend him, but they weren't there. Usually, the posse traveled together, and he was sure they would have given their two cents. Chris's supporters were nodding, sitting back in their seats, satisfied with the debate's outcome. Professor Hines waited patiently, but no one raised their hands. The professor had a smile on his face. He liked the arguments, the opinions, and the passion his students brought to the issues. He hardly interrupted a good discussion but added points to their arguments to ensure accuracy.

"To your point, Chris, one thing must happen for the law to be overturned. People must organize to either propose new laws or overturn old laws. Civil Rights Legislation was passed because people organized. Voting Rights Legislation passed because people organized. The drug laws will be overturned completely when people organize."

He then turned to Tommy. "And Tommy, your point about historical support for the laws was valid, but you let your opponent get away with stating that the laws ceased to be relevant and that the current argument was that the only way to make neighborhoods safe was to lock everybody up." Professor Hines laughed, and so did Tommy. "Overall, you both did very well and will be great lawyers someday."

Chris looked over at the classroom door and saw two of his boys from the Black Student Union—Barry and DJ—signaling for him to come out. Chris waved them off, but they kept motioning urgently for him to join them. Chris looked at Professor Hines, who had also seen his friends hovering at the door. Chris asked if he could be excused.

"You came in late, and now you want to be excused?" Professor Hines blew out a frustrated breath. "Very well," he acquiesced, "but make it quick."

# CHAPTER SIX

Chris hurried to the door. As soon as he was within earshot, Barry said, "They're meeting right now to finalize Quad Jam! These assholes are trying to jerk us!"

Chris looked over and saw Nina standing in the hall behind his boys. Her presence added to the rising tension he felt at his friends sudden appearance. "Nina, what happened?"

She shook her head, panting, "Come with us! We'll explain on the way."

"Where are we going?" Before he could say another word, Nina and Barry pulled him by the arm and dragged him down the hall, explaining as they picked up the pace to a trot.

"The Quad Jam Committee is meeting, and they're trying to determine the final bands for Quad Jam," Nina said. "We need to get in there and get our spots; they only have two left."

"We can't let those assholes book all the bands. We determine our own music!" Barry yelled, breaking into a run.

As they were running, Chris realized he'd been played by Tommy and his cohorts. They had arranged the meeting for the day of the debate. They had Tommy show up in class while they finalized plans for Quad Jam. The Quad Jam Committee was composed of White students from the Student Government and representatives from other, primarily White, organizations. Although the Black Student Union was supposed to have a representative on the committee, the committee never informed the BSU of the meetings, and unfortunately, the Black students never really paid attention to the meeting dates or times. They figured the Student Government had all the votes locked up, and their voices wouldn't matter, so they allowed the majority to determine all the acts for Quad Jam.

Chris's father had often told him, "Never allow anyone to represent your interest. You know best what your interest is."

In previous years, the Black students rebelled by having their own parties in another part of the campus and ignoring Quad Jam completely. But this year was different, Chris was graduating, and he encouraged the BSU to use Quad Jam as a means to an end, to publicize the demands of Black students.

While others cared about the music, Chris and his crew cared about the institution of Black faculty and Black departments to represent their interests in the future. There was a good chance there would be a band that the Black students could support.

White folks love Black music; they just don't love Black voices, Black demands, or Black history. The Black Student Union didn't want music for a day; they wanted Black professors teaching every day, in every class and every department on campus. He hoped to get bands on the stage to be active in that fight and amplify their voice.

This meeting was important, and he and others in the BSU had planned to attend.

How it worked was that the committee selected the bands and sent them to the dean for confirmation and budget approval. There were twelve spots; each band was allocated an hour to perform. When his boys heard of the committee meeting, eleven spots had been taken and confirmed. However, they'd gotten a tip from one of the White girls on the committee, who was dating a guy from the BSU, that there were now *two* slots left. One of the bands had dropped out, and with the other up for grabs, they had a chance to lay claim to the two remaining spots.

The secret meeting was being held on the ground floor of Founder's Hall in a back room. Chris and his crew ran through the hall and burst inside, to the apparent consternation of those already present. Their little group was clearly not welcomed, but they had a right to be present and heard. Since Chris was the president of the Black Student Union, he spoke up, more than a little out of breath.

"Good morning. Pardon our tardiness, but we came to get the last two spots."

One of the committee members jumped up from the table. "You can't just bust in here and make demands," he sneered. "That's not how it's done." Chris recognized him immediately as Jerry, one of Tommy's boys and a member of his debate crew.

Chris called him on it. "Jerry, you missed class this morning. Does Professor Hines know that you're here? I'll be sure to tell him you're in the basement planning secret meetings while class is in session. Anyway, we're part of this committee, and we want our spots. You all have ten of them, and we want the last two for our own bands."

"Too bad," Jerry smirked. "Looks like there's only one spot left."

"Look, we know that your last group dropped out. You guys never filled the spot, so that makes two. Did you skip math class today, too?" Everyone laughed at that remark, including his team.

Mark Jacobs, president of the committee, urged Jerry to sit down. He answered the demand in a reasonable tone, trying to appease everyone. "Excuse me, Chris, but he's right. We have only one spot left. We finalized the dropped spot right before you got here. And, if I may say, it's a Black band from New Orleans. Raymond spoke to them directly, so we do have a Black band as part of the celebration."

Raymond was a skinny, goofy, Black kid who hung with the White students and dated only White girls. He was known to many Black students as Uncle Ray, after Uncle Tom, because he was such a sellout. He didn't like Chris, nor did he like the BSU as an organization. He thought it was stupid to organize or even celebrate Black History Month, calling it unfair to other races and saying that Black people were the only race that had a month.

He and Chris had discussed the issue, but he disagreed with Chris's argument that White people had eleven months to push their history and agenda. He called Chris a reverse racist for heading the Black Student Union. He thought Black students should go along with what the school offered and forget about trying to hire Black professors or get an African American Studies Department. He believed activism led to separatism and hatred between the races.

To Chris, people like Uncle Ray were dangerous to the advancement of justice and equality. They were worse than racist White people. Their self-loathing led to them denying their own culture, history and–worst of all–the progress made during the Civil Rights Movement. They tried to ignore race, which Chris thought was inherently dangerous and stupid. Ray had no idea how much of a victim he was. Chris felt sorry for him, but there were others, Barry among them, who wanted to whip his ass.

Before Mark could say anything further, Barry jumped all over him. "Who the hell cares about Uncle Ray! He doesn't represent us; he represents his masters."

Raymond looked at him with disdain but said nothing. He feared Barry.

"You have a shitty Black band that *you* chose, not us," Barry continued his tirade. "We want to choose our own bands! What do you think this is, slavery—where you choose for us? Those days are over." Some of the members shifted in their seats like children being scolded. Chris took advantage of their discomfort at being called to account.

DJ calmed Barry down while Chris repeated the demands to the committee.

When the committee didn't answer, DJ chimed in. "Yo, you better give us those spots or I'm going to let my boy go. Believe me. Barry will bite your asses like a pitbull. Y'all help me. We don't need blood on this campus." DJ jokingly held Barry back.

Barry wasn't amused. "We will shut this shit down right now!" Barry demanded while pointing his fingers harshly at them.

The threat made the committee members bristle, and Chris felt they were losing ground as everyone around the table started to speak up, but it was Nina who finally got their attention.

"What about Black women artists?" Nina challenged them all.

Everyone, even Barry and DJ, was silent. They seemed to be listening to her. "You guys clearly do not represent all African Americans on this campus with the music. How many of the bands are Black women? There are a lot of them you could have called, but you missed that opportunity. Give us a spot so that we can find some Black female artists to represent our campus women."

"This meeting is to determine who we will invite, not to do more research to find bands to propose. That was supposed to have been done before this," Jerry said. Nina looked frustrated, but Chris took advantage of the confusion she had caused to jump in and use the same strategy the committee president had just used.

To play for time, he quickly jumped on a procedural point. "You all are operating against the charter. Twenty people are supposed to be on this committee—two representatives from each campus organization and a chairperson appointed by those on the committee. At least half of the members and the chairperson are supposed to be present for a quorum. You have eight people present. How are you voting without a quorum?"

No one replied. Chris raised a brow in challenge. "Either give us that spot, or we get technical and take two." He had obviously thrown them for a loop. They stared at Chris and his crew in confusion and concern. Chris wasn't sure he could require them to give them the spots, but he knew that in any political organization, a quorum is necessary to proceed with voting.

Mark asked that the committee members be given a minute to talk amongst themselves. Chris hesitated before nodding assent. Mark had always been a reasonable guy but could also be conniving. He was someone who smiled in your face but could also stab you in your back—a real politician. While Chris knew better than to trust him completely, he was always cordial and willing to publicly listen to other people's opinions. It was a gamble, but Chris thought they might just win it.

There were eight members of the Student Government at the table and four from the Black Student Union. Mark asked Chris and his crew to step out of the room. They didn't move, opting instead to stand up and move away but stay in the room while they conferenced in low voices.

"One minute up," Barry was all too happy to interrupt the proceedings.

"Come on, guys, we're trying here," Mark responded.

"Well talk fast because I gotta go to the bathroom, and I will shit on this floor right here if this takes too long," DJ joked.

Chris gave them another minute, but they took two more.

The decision was made. They turned around and looked at Chris and his group.

Mark spoke, "After a committee conference, we have decided that you can select the band for the open spot. We will forward your suggestion to the dean for confirmation."

Chris asked them if the secretary was recording the session. Mark answered yes. Chris asked to hear the recording, and the secretary read it aloud. Chris asked to hear the vote and learned that six had been in favor of their demands with one opposition and one abstention. Chris asked them to add his name and Barry's name to the vote in favor of the motion since they had made the proposal to the committee. That made it eight in favor, one opposed, and one abstention. The greater the margin in favor, the more likely the dean would be to approve the band.

Chris asked that the minutes reflect the changes in votes and be read again. After the vote was read aloud again, Chris and his crew left on a cordial note. Mark asked that they select their nominee for the final Quad Jam band as quickly as possible.

"Thank you for your time, ladies and gentlemen. We'll see you at Quad Jam. And Jerry, I'll see you in class." Chris said. Barry and DJ postured and grumbled at the committee, but Nina smiled and waved goodbye.

"Who the hell told them about this meeting?" Chris heard Jerry whine as they left the room.

Chris and his crew made their way down the hall, grinning, and by the time they reached the end of it, they were laughing, "Did you see their faces, them White boys looked shook." Barry smirked.

"Yeah, Barry, I should have let you beat someone's ass. Knock his ass right out for our ancestors' sakes," DJ stated.

Nina was still chattering in excitement, "Yeah, but we gotta consider a Black female artist. That would be historic."

Chris caught up to Nina and held her close. "Don't worry," he said, pressing a kiss to her lips. "It'll work out."

# CHAPTER SEVEN

With all the excitement, Chris had forgotten about leaving class early and had to run back to get his bag. When he returned, Professor Hines was in the classroom alone, grading papers.

"Sorry about earlier, Professor." He winced as he met his mentor's considering gaze. "There was an emergency."

"Just don't let it happen again." Professor Hines looked at him over the glasses he pushed down on his nose and offered Chris a quick smile. "With that being said, I'm glad you made it back. It gives me the chance to applaud you on your debate skills."

"Thanks." Chris walked up to the desk to get his bag to hand in his paper.

"You remind me of myself when I was younger." The Professor mused. "Bold, smart, and passionate about the issues. However, you must remember to balance your activism and academics. Each has its place—one is theoretical and the other practical, and in the real world, you'll have to deal with practical matters with a theoretical understanding. You want to show the world that you are not just an activist running after the issues but a disciplined, learned individual with proven knowledge of the matter at hand. The combination of scholarly discipline and perpetual activism could get you to the White House. As Abraham Lincoln once said, *'Whatever you are, be a good one.'*"

He shook Chris's hand. "Thank you, sir. You've been an inspiration to me."

As he was leaving, Chris thought about his statement. W.E. B. Du Bois, Adam Clayton Powell, Jr., Thurgood Marshall, and the Reverend Dr. Martin Luther King, Jr. were educated activists. They used the knowledge they gained in the academy to fight on behalf of Black people, poor people, and the disenfranchised. They earned people's respect. That's how Chris wanted to be. He wanted to be an educated activist. The person who had book knowledge and street smarts. The person who had respect in the boardroom because of his credentials and respect in the Black community because of his background in the hood.

But balancing the two, plus maintaining a private life, would be his biggest challenge. It was already proving to be as much as he could handle, juggling his social life, student representative responsibilities, and classwork. He planned to graduate with honors, though. That was his top priority for college and getting accepted into law school.

Chris met up with Nina, and they hurried to the cafeteria to meet with Barry and DJ.

"How did the debate go?" Nina asked.

"I nailed it." Chris assured her, "Sent that racist back to the pits of hell." Nina kissed him, and they made their way to the cafeteria.

DJ and Barry were waiting there, and Chris told them to assemble a group of students from the Black Student Union so they could begin organizing their nomination for a band for Quad Jam. Barry was most excited about the event. Even though he was in college, his goal was to be a big-time hip-hop artist. He sold his mixtapes on campus and was the resident rapper. He also had a show on the campus radio station, which was so good even people off-campus listened to it. Whenever the BSU had a party, he was the one to organize it. On weekends he hung around the clubs with up-and-coming artists who were looking for their break. Barry made a couple of calls to some friends but didn't get any bites.

Sheila showed up while they were talking alternatives. Sheila was the vice president of the Union, and she had the most beautiful soul that Chris had ever known, always willing to go all out for her friends. She was bright as hell, too.

"Hey everybody, what's going on? You all look like we ready to tear this campus up."

"We are," Nina assured her. "We just got a spot for Quad Jam and we're trying to get a famous group to perform."

*Free Nina: The College Years*

"What! Yes!" Sheila was ecstatic. "How about if I ask my dance group to be a part of the program." Sheila was a dancer with an African dance company in the city. "They won't cost us anything but time."

"That sounds like an interesting possibility," Chris answered. It would be good if the dancers didn't charge a fee because all the money would go to the band if they found one.

Sheila's major was dance and drama, and even though the school wasn't big on either, she was able to design her own major and have it approved by the dean. Sheila was articulate and witty and always strictly business. She knew how to cut to the chase and get the job done. She suggested, "Why don't we get a Black choir from one of the local churches to join with our gospel choir from the school as part of the program."

"Sounds good. Will you coordinate?" Chris asked. She nodded.

"If we got a famous rapper, we would give him the last half hour of our one-hour spot with the dancers and the choir at the top of the hour." Sheila jumped at it.

"What up! What y'all doin?" David interrupted the meeting. They nicknamed him Wannabe, and he accepted the name without complaint. Wannabe was a skinny blond kid who wanted to be Black, thus the name Wannabe. He was always hanging around Black students, particularly Barry and Chris – radical as they were in dealing with the administration. Whenever they met with the administration to discuss hiring more Black teachers, Wannabe was there. Wannabe was cool but annoying. An adopted kid from a wealthy family in Westchester County, he was an outcast, mostly because he was too hip-hoppish for his family, who would have preferred he hang out with his own kind. Or rather, with their kind. Wannabe had connections to the music industry through his family, and Chris knew if they asked him for something, he could be counted on to do it.

Barry asked him to get in contact with one of the rap groups the BSU was considering, and Wannabe was on it. They all walked him back to his room, where he called his uncle, who worked for a law firm that represented rappers. His uncle told him he would get back to him and Wannabe insisted that he do so no later than 5:00 p.m. Chris and the others laughed at the tone he took with his family. Still, they included him in the razzing and carried him along with them as they headed back to the cafeteria.

It was decided that Barry would be the rapper's contact person if Wannabe came through. In the meantime, Chris would work on making sure the dean confirmed their band and that the funding came through. Chris told them that whatever rapper they got, they had to ensure they had a decent reputation. They couldn't bring anyone to the event that would cuss and promote violence, especially against women, even though it was commonplace. Nina hated some of the lyrics, even of the most popular rappers.

Barry wasn't going for it. He felt the other bands had no restrictions on them, so why should the rappers? "The rock bands that come to campus don't give a damn," Barry argued. "They promote drinking and drugs in your face. If anybody should be censored and monitored, it should be them. Rappers only talk shit; they don't all live that way."

"Nah, Barry, I'm even scared of some of them rap dudes, talking about raping hoes and killing cops. The way some of them dudes look makes me want to run." DJ stated as he shook his head in agreement.

Nina chimed in, "We need some women rappers or even R&B artists. At least they won't promote that gangster stuff, and we don't have to worry about violence."

Sheila jumped in as well. "Yeah, we don't need those thug asses up here. Gangster rappers attract other street ghetto asses, and then we'll be seen as defeating our purpose and messing up Quad Jam if anything goes wrong. Even if the rock bands do their drugs, they don't shoot up shit at the parties. We need to make sure we invite someone political and mainstream who can help us get our message across."

Since 1988, plenty of rap music had emerged that was more socially and politically conscious than the gangster and party rap that had been popular early on. Public Enemy was at the top of the list. They released a string of radical hits that challenged White power, government inequality, and the media. They were on their fourth album, and there was no stopping them. Everyone, including White people, sang their lyrics. "Yo! Bum Rush the Show," "Fight the Power," and "Don't Believe the Hype" were all popular around campus. They would be great for the cause.

Another rap group, N.W.A., was dominating the West Coast and making waves with violent rhymes and radical lyrics about "Fuck the Police." The song was a major hit and put West Coast rappers on the map with East Coast rappers. They were good but maybe a little too controversial for this event.

A third powerful force in East Coast rap was KRS-One. He was from The Bronx, raised not far from Chris. He had dominated the scene with his 1987 and 1988 albums and now was on the lecture circuit at colleges around the nation, speaking about injustice and the inequality of Black people. He used his albums to catapult him from rapper to university lecturer without a college degree. He would have been the best choice for Quad Jam; he was politically educated and referred to as the 'teacha' who kicked knowledge.

The Wu-Tang Clan from Staten Island, Eric B and Rakim from Long Island and Slick Rick the storyteller might work, but getting any of the artists, Chris knew, would be difficult at this late date and expensive. But they could only try.

"You're all right, but let's make sure we represent ourselves on a higher level," Chris said. "This is more than entertainment for us; it's about campus justice that we're trying to get across." He turned to Barry and Wannabe, "Just get someone that will make us look good, so we can make sure our voices are heard when the band leaves the stage."

"Just don't forget about Black women artists; they should be considered, too." Nina persisted in her campaign.

Barry came at her. "Oh, here you go with that Black woman mess again. You almost divided us in front of that committee today. Give that shit a rest. They ain't even no Black female rappers out there."

Chris was about to jump in and confront Barry about how he spoke to Nina, but before he could, Nina was defending herself very effectively.

"I didn't divide anything." She snapped. "I was just letting them know we had bands—including female groups—that we wanted to support." Nina moved towards him. "You so-called brothers' forget about Black women. That's why there are hardly any Black women in the rap game, except for sisters like MC Lyte and Queen Latifah, who are just as good, if not better than some of those dudes. But you nasty men just want to use women for dancing half-naked in your videos and sex, like we're floor mats to be stepped on. It's a shame how White and Black men disrespect and degrade Black women." Nina was in his face now, and though her expression was light, almost playful, her words were serious. Sheila jumped in to support her, and Barry backed down, figuring he had been outnumbered.

"You better watch your ass," Chris warned Barry, only half-joking. He just looked aside.

"Oh Snap, Barry, you were about to get that ass whipped by some women." DJ laughed as Barry threw up his hands in either surrender or frustration.

"Yo, shut up!" Barry pushed DJ as he doubled over laughing, and they all laughed at both guys.

Chris ended the argument, suggesting they continue planning and organizing for the rest of the day. They would meet in his dorm room tomorrow afternoon to report on any new developments.

"I have class tomorrow at that time, so I'll be a little late," Sheila responded.

Chris said, "No problem, just keep in touch with DJ, who will be your assistant."

DJ squinted his eyes at Chris and responded, "Assistant. I ain't no assistant. I'm the treasurer. I count money, digits, dollars dude. 'Cash Rules Everything Around Me, Cream. Get The Money. Dollar dollar bill, y'all.'" DJ busted one of the lyrics from The Wu-Tang Clan.

"I was just joking, but that brings up another good point. We need you to come up with some ways for us to make money for the Black Student Union at Quad Jam." DJ knew how to get the job done, especially when it came to money, which was why he was the treasurer of the Black Student Union. In addition, he was a good assistant and faithful in his service to Barry, Sheila and Chris.

*Free Nina: The College Years*

Barry and DJ were great friends and roommates and were hardly ever seen without each other. Both were juniors, and since Chris was about to graduate, he had prioritized mentoring them so they could take over the Black Student Union the following year.

Chris had been president since sophomore year and had learned a lot about the politics of the students, alumnae, faculty, and administration. Barry would begin his presidency in September when he returned from summer break, and DJ would be his vice president. DJ liked Sheila, who was also a junior, and definitely didn't mind working with her, no matter what he said. Sometimes Chris thought the only reason he was part of the Black Student Union was that Sheila was second in command.

Sheila, however, was too much into her dancing to worry about guys. She had been hurt by love when a former boyfriend got a woman from campus pregnant and married her after graduation last year. Since then, she hadn't dated, but she excelled in everything she did. She always said to Chris and Nina that her ex-boyfriend would regret leaving her for another woman.

Chris shook his head, focusing on the meeting once more. "One last thing. No one say a word to anyone until we have everything confirmed. We want to look efficient and effective and impress everybody with what we can do."

He reminded them all of the importance of moving quickly. "We only have three days until the resurrection," he pointed out.

Sheila and DJ would work on the African dancers, the choir, and coordinating the program. Barry and Wannabe would work on the rapper, while Nina would help Barry and Wannabe consider a female rapper or R & B singer for the show. "Meanwhile, I will work on the dean to secure our funding." He always liked to recap at the end of meetings for clarity. He waited for everyone to signal they heard and understood, and then he reached out to them. They put their fists on top of his, looked at each other, and cried JUSTICE! That was how the meetings adjourned. Then they all went their separate ways.

---

Nina and Chris walked back to her room. As they walked, Nina again brought up the subject of the female performers.

"So, Chris, what do you think about female rappers or an R & B artist performing at Quad Jam? You haven't said anything, and you know if you say it, Wannabe and Barry will check into it."

"I did say something. I told Barry and Wannabe to work with you to consider a female artist."

Nina pulled at his shirtfront, bringing him to a stop and holding him still as she looked up into his face. "No, Chris, I mean you didn't give your opinion on the matter. You didn't state that we need to do this. You know that if you said it, Barry and Wannabe would do it."

"Nina, truthfully." He said as calmly as he could while looking Nina in her eyes. "Like Barry said, that's dead. I mean, those female rappers and R & B singers can't bring the noise like male rappers can. White folks don't respect them. They're just entertainers with no real political message. I mean, it's not like they're Marvin Gaye, who had a social message in the music. Most of these singers and female rappers are all about love and unity. That'll be playday for the administration, just another song and dance like we're some clowns. We need someone to blast this White establishment and racist campus and get the message out. We've been trying to get respect on this campus for years, and to bring female artists up here wouldn't accomplish that goal." Chris wanted her to understand his position, even though he knew she would disagree.

"Ok, forget it," Nina said heatedly as she let go of his shirt and turned away. "I see you have your mind made up. I just think any Black entertainer that came up here could send a message, and a female would not only break down racial barriers but gender barriers as well." Nina started walking swiftly, obviously frustrated.

"Come on, Nina." Chris jumped in front of her, stopping her in her tracks in his turn and grabbing her by the hands as she dropped her head to avoid meeting his pleading eyes. "You know what we're trying to do here. This is not about a song and dance or a good time; this is about change. We don't need Black entertainers; we need game-changers. We need a change on this campus. I'm doing this for you and all the women on campus. You will be here next semester. I'm graduating. I just want to see some changes before I leave. I like female artists and all, but seriously Nina, if we want to send a message and get this school's attention, we need Black radical indignation, which can only come through rappers who earnestly confront this racist nation." Chris was as surprised as she was at the unintentional rhymes that came out of his mouth and the rhythmic cadence of his speech.

"Oh, you a rapper now," Nina said with a laugh as she finally looked up at him. "If we don't get anybody, maybe you should just get up there and perform. I'm sure you'll be great at it." He smiled, embarrassed but happy that she seemed to have loosened up.

Nina stared into his eyes for a searching moment. "Ok, I get it. Let's do what we must do to make this a success." Chris hugged and kissed Nina as they continued to walk back to her room, knowing that she was still not pleased with the decision but willing to trust his judgment on the matter. Nina went into her room and closed the door behind her after they kissed good night. Chris jogged back down the hallway, eager to plan his next move.

## CHAPTER EIGHT

"**H**ey girlfriend, you ok? I'm running to class in a few." Tracy said, jumping up to make her bed as Nina entered the room.

"Give it up, Tracy. You'll just be getting under the covers in a couple of hours."

She put the pillow down and came towards Nina, looking a bit guilty, until she saw her roommate's face. "Oh no, looks like you and Chris had a little disagreement. What's up?"

"Nothing big," Nina stated as she slowly made her way over to her bed and laid down as if she were exhausted.

Tracy sat next to her on the single bed. "What happened this morning when Barry dragged you out of here?" Tracy asked curiously.

Nina quickly rose from her prone position. "Well, The Quad Jam Committee has a couple of spots, and they were trying to fill them before we could, but we were able to secure one spot. I suggested a female rapper or female R&B artist, and Barry and his crazy ass disagreed with me, and Chris is taking his side. Telling me that *'female artists aren't strong enough to gain respect on this campus and tear down the establishment.'"* Nina said as she mimicked Chris's voice. "I totally disagree." She continued. "Any Black artists who come up here, male or female, could be used to challenge the establishment. A Black female artist would not only challenge the racist system but the sexist system as well, being as we have no Black women in any position of power on this campus. All we have to do is tell the artist what we're trying to do and allow them to use their influence to confront the school. Don't you agree?"

Nina looked at Tracy for an affirmative response. "Well, did you tell Chris that?" Tracy inquired, avoiding the trap of being forced to take sides for or against her roommate's boyfriend.

"I tried, but you know Chris, it's either his way or the highway when it comes to race matters. He's not always on board with women's issues. He's a typical Black man when it comes to the feminist cause. Besides, I just don't have the energy to fight with him and miss an opportunity to challenge the hegemony and bigotry on this campus. The racism on this campus is deeply ingrained, and like Chris said, we need to topple it. There will be other opportunities to add the womanist perspective and get our presence and demands on the agenda, particularly next year when Chris graduates and I'm still here. So, if Chris believes we can change things with male rappers, then I'll go along with it, whether I agree with him or not."

"Ok, but you must learn to use your feminist voice too," Tracy advised cautiously.

"Believe me, I do. You should have seen how I came at Barry." Nina said, standing and balling up her fists. "I was about to punch him in his face. He's always trying to bully somebody. I'm from The Bronx. I ain't scared of his little Brooklyn self."

Tracy and Nina laughed, and Tracy said, "Cool it girl, you don't want to hurt nobody with that Bronx style of yours. Use it to give Chris all that loving he's been missing."

"Yeah, but Chris is my man and you know I stick by my man. Like Salt and Peppa said, 'What a man, what a man, what a man. What a mighty good man." Nina sang as she went towards the bathroom.

"I do. You are one supportive woman of your man. Let's just hope you always get the support you need as well." Nina looked back at Tracy from the bathroom doorway and raised her eyebrows. "I don't plan to settle for anything less." Nina smiled.

"You shouldn't. I'm here to help you fight the good fight."

"I appreciate that, roomie. Thanks."

# CHAPTER NINE

Chris woke up to rain the next day. He didn't know if this was a good sign or a portent of gloom. He got dressed, threw on his black hoodie — the one he usually wore in The Bronx to blend in with the guys in the hood — and ran across the quad to the castle where the faculty and administrative offices were. The workers had built part of the stage for Quad Jam but had stopped because of the rain. He ran to the dean's office to speak with him about the funding for the band. Chris knew the dean came in at 8:00 a.m. every morning, and since he didn't have an appointment, he planned to meet him at the door upon arrival. They walked into the building at the same time.

"Just the person I want to see," Chris said, stopping him.

The dean jumped back. "Oooh Christopher, you scared me." It must have been the black hoodie.

"How are you?" he cleared his throat, then said in his most professional tone. "Are you here to talk about us hiring Black faculty? We're working on it and have started setting up some interviews next week to begin hiring for September. I told my secretary to send you a notice about the interviews. Did you get it?"

Dean Martin knew Chris well. He was the dean of academics and campus organizations and was on the steering committee to hire more African American faculty at the school. Chris was the president of the Black Student Union and was part of the committee. Since freshman year, the BSU urged the committee to hire more African American faculty and develop an African American Studies Department. There was only one tenured African American faculty member at the school and that was in the Art Department. The other African American faculty were all adjunct professors, which meant they were temporary and were only guaranteed positions for a semester or two. The turnover in the positions was high. They tended to come and go. More Black tenure-track professors were needed in departments such as religion, sociology, psychology, and political science.

Tenure-track employment gave professors security and stability in their academic careers as long as they met the requirements in their discipline. Manhattanville College had not hired a single tenure-track African American professor in the four years that Chris had attended. The administration, including the school president, had assured the Black Student Union that they would see real change this year, and Chris wanted to make sure they fulfilled their promise before he graduated. So far, nothing had changed. The administration knew how to play politics. Chris was sure they planned to appease the BSU with measures to make it *seem* like they were working to satisfy their demands without actually making any changes.

They allowed Chris, in his capacity as the President of the Black Student Union, to interview candidates for tenure positions, suggest courses for an African American Studies Department, advertise employment positions in Black newspapers, and volunteer on the steering committee. None of these efforts ever materialized into anything. The administration knew they could stall until his four years were up, and then when he graduated, the next BSU president would have to start the process all over again. Just as the class before him had done and the class before that. With the students constantly changing, they couldn't maintain the fight from one graduating class to the next, so the administration got away with half-assed efforts, resulting in no new tenure-track Black faculty members being hired.

"Yes, I got it," Chris said with a decided lack of enthusiasm as he pulled the hood of his sweatshirt down from over his head.

"Good. Is there anything else I can do for you?" Dean Martin managed to remain formal and polite while speed-walking toward his office.

Chris didn't have a personal problem with Dean Martin; he seemed to be a fair and just guy regarding BSU's concerns. It was just that his hands were tied. He could only do so much without consulting the highest authorities, but he always tried to help.

"I'm here about a different matter, though I would like to discuss the faculty issue later after meeting the applicant." The dean seemed both relieved and anxious, a complex expression to achieve. Chris matched his fast pace walking down the hall and up the stairs. "Have you approved the Quad Jam Committee's request for the final band?"

The dean frowned slightly, "Actually, I haven't seen it yet."

Right there, Chris's heart stopped. What if Mark and Jerry never submitted the request, or if they were holding on to it so time and funding could run out? It wouldn't surprise him. Mark was a snake, and Jerry was a jerk.

"What do you mean you didn't see it?" Chris tried to control his annoyance and keep his voice even, but it was hard, especially as they jog-walked up the stairs. Breathing heavily, he stopped at the bend halfway up the staircase. Leaning in toward his surprised face, Chris spoke through gritted teeth, "Mark said he would get it to you. We finalized it yesterday."

"I didn't see it," he repeated dismissively and started walking up the final stairs to his office. Chris followed, stumped and frustrated. Dean Martin stopped at his office door and looked him straight in the eyes. "Look, it's getting late, and to be truthful Chris, how can you expect to find a band in just two days?"

"Did you ask the committee that when they said they were still looking for a band for the final slot?" he asked. It wasn't the point whether the BSU could find someone more quickly or as quickly as they could. The Quad Jam Committee was obligated to give the dean the information.

Chris was getting angrier, his heartbeat echoing in his eardrums, both from their run through the building and from the rage he felt building at the disrespect to the BSU and himself. Luckily, just as he was about to turn and leave, seething with anger at Mark Jacobs for his action, the dean said. "Wait, let me check with my secretary. I might have missed it, or she might have forgotten to give it to me." Chris followed him through the outer door of his office suite. As they walked into the room, his secretary greeted him. "Did anything come in from the Quad Jam Committee?" he asked. She ignored Chris, who stood just behind him, looking over his shoulder as he shuffled through the pile of papers she handed him. He looked through it swiftly, finally pulling out a letter from the Student Government with Mark's signature on it.

Chris visibly sagged in relief that he wasn't going to fight this battle again. Mark would have had to be crazy to jerk them around like that. Dean Martin moved the request to the top of the stack and looked at the form as he walked through the secretary's office, went through another door into his own office, and sat down at his desk. Chris continued to follow him and sat in one of the chairs facing him, waiting eagerly for his response.

He finally raised his head. "I don't see the name of the band here. What is their name?" He asked with a concerned expression.

"We're still working on that, and they will call us today to confirm," Chris said as he stood and moved towards his desk.

"But Christopher, I need a name. How can I sign off without a name? You have to get me something, or I can't approve it. And if you can't-"

"Their name is KRSONE/PUBLICENEMY," he interrupted, putting the possible names together as one group. He had no idea whether either would come through, but it was worth bluffing to get the signature they needed. Chris assumed Dean Martin had no idea about rap music. The only music ever heard in his office was classical, which Chris also enjoyed. The dean asked him to write down the group's name on the request form, which he did. Dean Martin then quickly signed off on it.

Finally, Chris asked the question he had come to ask. "How much money do we have to secure the group?"

He smiled proudly. "We have budgeted five thousand dollars, but you need to get a contract to me immediately. Today."

"I will get it to you." Chris had no idea how any of this would happen, but he spoke as if it were no problem. His mother had always said to walk with faith. In other words, walk and talk like things will work in your favor even if you don't know how."

Chris was beginning to understand what she meant.

He thanked the dean, who stood up and extended his hand. Chris shook it.

"I hope you get Public Enemy," he quipped, mischief in his eyes. "I like their songs better."

Shocked, all Chris could do was laugh as he ran out of his office and through the secretary's office, out the door, and down the stairs.

He burst through the doors, and instead of waiting until noon, he ran through the quad straight to Wannabe's room. Chris needed to know if there'd been any developments. Things were moving fast, and there was no time to waste. Wannabe opened the door as soon as Chris banged on it, wearing nothing on but shorts. His oily blond hair fell over his face, and his skeletal body was disgustingly pale as if he were ill.

"Damn dude, I thought you were the po-po. What's up?" Wannabe asked, scratching his head and wiping his eyes simultaneously. His breath stunk like he'd been smoking weed, which he was known to do.

"You got any news? We need to move on this. The dean signed off on our request, and we have a budget of up to five thousand dollars, but he needs the contract today at the latest."

"I think we're good. I have Public Enemy in the works." Chris's eyes lit up. This was good news.

"What do you mean, in the works?" Chris asked excitedly.

"I mean, my uncle is working on them. He said he would call me back by 10:00 to finalize things."

## Free Nina: The College Years

"Well, it's 9:30. Call your uncle," Chris demanded, impatient. He made the phone call. His uncle picked up, and Chris heard through the receiver, "Good news." David was nodding and giving his visitor the thumbs up as he walked over to the desk to write down the details, and it was clear they had secured Public Enemy to play at Quad Jam. Chris started silently jumping and mouthing, "Holy shit! We did it!" Wannabe was still half-asleep, and Chris hissed at him to get the contract faxed over right away. They couldn't afford to screw this up. When his uncle agreed to send it, Chris instructed him to have his name put on the cover letter. Wannabe hung up the phone, and Chris smacked Wannabe on the chest, thrilled. "Good job!" Before he could respond, Chris raced back to the dean's office to wait for the contract.

As he ran across the lawn, he noticed that the rain had stopped, and the sun was bursting through the clouds. A promising sign, especially since work was being restarted on the stage for Quad Jam.

When he arrived at Dean Martin's office, the secretary was holding the contract.

"Is this for you, Christopher?" she said sarcastically.

"Yes. Thank you."

"No problem. Just remember this is Dean Martin's Office, not Christopher Raine's office." She handed it to him, and he rolled his eyes at the attitude. Her old ass was nasty to all the students, so he ignored her. He was happy to know that he'd gotten the contract and that Public Enemy would be their band for Quad Jam.

Chris went in search of Nina and told her they'd gotten Public Enemy. Chris was proud of what they had accomplished. She seemed impressed, but she wasn't as excited as he was.

"Oh, that's great," Nina said with a reluctant smile. "But I still think Queen Latifah would have done it, too. But all is good." Nina rewarded him with a hug and a big kiss, and Chris was satisfied.

# CHAPTER TEN

Later that afternoon, they met up with Sheila and the gang in his room as planned. Barry and DJ were ecstatic. They couldn't believe they would have their rap idols on campus. They could hardly contain themselves. Sheila had booked the African dance group and the local choir. She and Nina were going to meet with them the next day to coordinate the program. Their time slot was 3:00 to 4:00 p.m., and their band would be the seventh to perform. Four more groups were after them, including Mark's brother's band, which was playing last. He wanted them to close out the event as the best group at Quad Jam.

Most students loved Quad Jam at night. It was easier to get high, drunk, and have sex after dark, so the last performance was often the highlight. The Black New Orleans group was second to last, which the committee had apparently thought would appease the Black students.

They were all set. Chris told Barry and DJ that they had one more item to add to the agenda, and he would meet them tomorrow night before Quad Jam to go over it. In the meantime, they had to get the word out about Public Enemy coming to campus. DJ and Barry were good at spreading the news; they posted flyers all over campus and got on the campus radio station. Barry used the occasion to get his name out there too. He went on a few stations in New York City and invited local club promoters to the campus. DJ decided to make some money by selling T-shirts he had made. The shirts read "BSU/FIGHT THE POWER" in bright red letters on a black T-shirt. The proceeds would go to the Black Student Union so they wouldn't leave its coffers empty for the start of next semester.

Chris suggested that all the BSU leadership and volunteers wear the T-shirt on the day of Quad Jam. DJ agreed to make extra T-shirts for them at half price.

Chris called for a Black Student Union meeting that night. Nina oversaw coordinating the students once they came out. They needed help and support from all the Black students on campus to promote the event. They also wanted everyone to know they needed help applying pressure on the administration to hire Black faculty and an African American Studies Department.

When they got to the meeting, Chris was shocked. Chris had never seen so many students at a BSU meeting since his election as president. Usually, fifteen or twenty people attended, but over two hundred showed up that night. There were Black, White, Hispanic, Asian, and biracial students. There were even students who didn't like Chris because they thought he was too radical and a reverse racist prejudiced against White people. He had tried to explain that that was far from the truth. Chris always said that being pro-Black didn't mean he was anti-White. He was a loudmouth for low voices for those who wanted change. Nobody understood that more than a guy named Henry, whom he called Nicodemus. Nicodemus was a character in the bible that his father once told him about.

Nicodemus would sneak out at night and speak to Jesus about theological issues because he didn't want his followers, who were opposed to Jesus, to know. Henry was from Africa and was an *undercover activist*. He was part of the Black Student Union but also loved his White women. Henry met with Chris secretly to voice his support because he didn't want his White friends to think he was hanging with a Black radical. He was the one who let them know covertly about the secret meeting of The Quad Jam Committee. No matter how anyone felt about Chris before, everyone seemed to love him that night. Or at least they loved what he had to offer.

The meeting was so full they had to move it to the Student Game Room next door, which held about a hundred people. This was a room where students came to play pool, relax, and even do their work. They interrupted some students already using the space, but most were there for the BSU's planning meeting. The crowd overflowed into the lobby, and Chris stood on top of the pool table in the middle of the room and started to address the crowd. Barry, DJ, Nina, and Sheila stood in front of the pool table like bodyguards and calmed the crowd. When the room was relatively quiet, Chris spoke to them.

"Thank you all for coming out. I know you heard about Public Enemy coming to campus, which is why many of you are here."

Everyone began applauding as they stood up and shouted, "Public Enemy number one! Public Enemy number one! Public Enemy number one!"

Barry and DJ calmed the crowd once again as Chris raised his voice to address the whole congregation of students.

"In the past, the so-called Quad Jam Committee decided on the bands for us, but this year we decided who we wanted ourselves—and who we wanted was Public Enemy!" They applauded again.

One of the Black students he had seen before, but never met, said, "Yes! We decide!"

"This is not only about Public Enemy playing for Quad Jam. This is also about the Black Student Union being represented and our voices being heard on this campus. We need your help to make this a great event and make sure the administration hears us loud and clear: it's time to hire more tenure-track African American faculty."

"Yes!" the crowd erupted

"It's time to create an African American Studies Department."

"Yes!" They applauded again.

"It's time to get some Black women faculty on this campus!"

Nina turned around in surprise and appreciation with a smile at that last call as she began to clap and throw her fists in the air.

"Yes, yes!" The students applauded once more. The same kid shouted out one of Public Enemy's lyrics: "Fight the power, we got to fight the powers that be." Everyone began singing in unison with him. It lasted for about two minutes. Chris couldn't believe how the song—the great unifier—brought all these students together so fast. It was as if everyone on campus was on the same side for the first time. He took advantage of the opportunity to stir up the crowd.

"We not only need your help for Quad Jam, but we also need your help to make a change on this campus. Will you join me to fight the power for change? If you will, scream, 'Fight the power!'"

"Fight the power. We've got to fight the powers that be!" The crowd went wild, and this time it took longer for Barry and DJ to calm them again. Nina and Sheila joined them in quieting everyone down, but Chris didn't want to lose the energy. He turned around and saw campus security watching the crowd nervously. They didn't attempt to stop the speeches, just watched from a distance, probably because it was such a big crowd.

Chris continued with his plea. "I want to thank Barry, aka MC Barry Tone, and DJ, who will be BSU's president and vice president next semester." Applause again. "They need your help.

The administration has promised change, but they know we only have four years, so they stall for four years and wait until we graduate. Then they start the cycle all over again. But not this time. What I started and what those before me started, Barry and DJ will continue with your help. By next year, we want more faculty of color on this campus. Fight the power!"

"Fight the powers that be!" was the response.

"I also want to thank Sheila and my beautiful girlfriend Nina for coordinating the event. Because of them, this will be one of the greatest shows ever at Quad Jam." The cheers and applause swelled. Nina was clearly pleased and started waving her hand like she was the First Lady of the United States.

Feeling the energy and excitement, Nina and Sheila shouted: "All the ladies in the place say yeah—say yeah, yeah!" All the women yelled along with Nina and Sheila, who waved their hands.

"I also want to thank David for working with us to make all this possible. David is officially a Black man in White skin and a member of the Black Student Union as of today." Everyone laughed but then applauded even louder as Wannabe bowed to their applause.

"Now sign up to help and remember we have to fight the powers that be." Chris jumped down off the table. Barry turned on the music, blasting Public Enemy's song, and everyone sang and danced to "Fight the Power" as they lined up to help with Quad Jam. Nina was at her best, signing up students and encouraging women to get involved.

Meanwhile, DJ sold each person who signed up to volunteer a T-shirt for half price. "Get your T-shirts over here," he called. People flocked to him for the chance at a souvenir. They put on their shirts and left to let other students know that Public Enemy was coming to Manhattanville College.

At least a hundred students signed up to work at Quad Jam that night. They needed security guards, help coordinating the event, people to join the school's gospel choir, and others to spread the word off-campus. They had one day to do it all, but with the numbers that had shown up and the crowd's excitement, Chris had no doubt they would get all they needed.

Although the school would be swarming with security guards and police officers to prevent unauthorized people from getting in, they still wanted the public to know that the Black Student Union at Manhattanville College was doing something great. He wanted the name of Manhattanville College and the Black Student Union attached to the biggest event in Westchester County.

"Hey, Chris, look who came out to support us." It was Tracy.

"Congratulations!" Tracy said with a big smile, trying to give him a hug that he easily avoided.

"Chris, don't be mean." Nina hit him on his arm. "She came to support." Nina shot him a look of annoyance.

He gave Tracy a tight smile. "Thanks. Why don't you and some of your boyfriends help us get the word out?"

"Of course, I'll help, and yes, I have many guy friends who can help also," Tracy responded politely.

"That would be nice of you," he said sarcastically.

"Chris, she's going to help me get the word out."

"Ok, well, maybe she can help you with your grandmother early Saturday morning, and then you can get back by noon or one-ish. That way, you can get the groceries, and your grandmother won't worry about you because you didn't show up."

Nina usually went home on Saturdays to be with her grandmother and spent the day. Nina's grandmother was her sole guardian, and Nina did a great job taking care of her even while in school. Her grandmother was old, and though strong, she could be needy. Though demanding of Nina's time and energy, Nina did all that she could for her.

"Sure, I can do that," Tracy blurted out.

"No, I'm going to stay here Saturday. My grandma will be ok."

"Nina, the last time we went away for the weekend without telling her, she ended up in the hospital with heart palpitations, and we had to rush back and end our trip early. We can't leave the concert if she gets sick or worried."

"Well, if anything happens, I'll take care of it," Nina insisted blandly. In an indignant tone, she added. "And that was over a year ago. She's gotten better since then or worse because at times her dementia kicks in, and she doesn't know what day it is."

Nina hugged him, ignoring Tracy's presence; she looked somberly into his eyes. "I'm here for the event and for you. Don't I always help you? Aren't we a team?"

"Yes," he whispered back. "And I thank you, but all I'm saying is it would be good to visit her early to assure no interference on that day."

"Yeah, Nina, I can take you. It's no problem," Tracy interrupted.

Nina retorted shortly, "I said she'll be fine, Chris. If anything happens, I'll take care of it. Now let's work on the show."

"Will you at least call her in the morning to tell her you won't be coming? I know she's hard of hearing, but at least you will have warned her." Nina nodded, and Chris had to settle for that, even though, at times, her grandmother didn't pick up the phone.

He left Nina to her own devices and focused on Quad Jam, knowing that if something happened with her grandmother, it would mess everything up for the day, but there was nothing more he could do about it.

# CHAPTER ELEVEN

Chris was so excited he could hardly sleep. He woke up every hour on the hour. His soul was restless and anxious, his heart beat rapidly, and his mind wandered on the worst that could happen at Quad Jam today. At about 1:00 a.m., he went to Nina's room and told her to come over because he was restless. She said he could sleep in her bed with her, but Chris wasn't comfortable sleeping in her room with her roommate there.

Tracy had been Nina's roommate since freshman year, and they had secured a room for next semester, planning to live together as seniors. Nina believed that Chris didn't like Tracy because she was White. But actually, Chris didn't like Tracy because she was promiscuous. She dated too many guys, and he didn't think she was good for Nina. Although he trusted Nina wholeheartedly, her friend was too much of a freak for him. Chris convinced her to come over to his room. She made hot chocolate and gave him a massage that put him right to sleep.

When Chris woke up, the sun was shining gloriously. The rain the day before had paved the way for a luminous sky with no clouds in sight. The five-foot-tall, twenty-foot-deep stage was complete, and the sight made Chris think of a spaceship that had landed in the middle of the quad. The pillars that held up the screen were like stars in the sky, and music was already playing at 8:00 in the morning.

Many of the local groups went on early in the day. Although there wasn't much of an audience in the morning, the bands used the opportunity to invite family and friends to record the show so they could build up their portfolio within the music industry. At noon, more people began to assemble. This was usually when the first big act came out, and the quad was now teeming with students and journalists. The parking lots were already full, and security had to direct people to park in a lot at the other end of the campus. Special guests like the VIPs that Barry invited were given passes to attend. The bands used a private entrance and were assigned a security guard to escort them to the stage. A trailer was set up to house the bands until it was their time to perform.

Security was tight and abundant. Chris had never seen so many police officers. He began to wonder if that was for safety or if they anticipated trouble because so many Black people were showing up on campus. So many officers would only incite a riot, not prevent one. However, he stayed calm, assuming that everything would work out.

He went to the gym where Nina and Sheila were coordinating the dancers and choir. Everyone looked good. Sheila introduced Chris to her dance instructor, Ms. Shepherd. She was an older woman with a great body and beautiful Black skin. It is true when they say, 'Black don't crack.' She must have been seventy years old with not one wrinkle or blemish on her face. Chris greeted her with a warm kiss on the cheek, and she blushed.

"So, you're the famous president of the BSU. Sheila talks about you all the time," she said.

Chris was taken by the woman's voice, which sang like a C note when she spoke.

"You can't believe everything you hear," he responded. Chris told her how beautiful she was and how much Sheila loved and admired her. He even put in a plug for Sheila by suggesting she get her solo in their next big show. That was Sheila's dream. She wanted to dance, act, and sing on Broadway.

The choir was also working hard. Chris met the choir director, a chubby dude with a small head. Upon meeting Chris, he blurted out a note, and everyone began to laugh. He waved to the choir members, and they sang in unison, "Hello, Mr. President."

Chris felt like the President of the United States. The church pastor had come along to see his choir perform, and the director introduced him to Chris as Pastor Brian Hill of the White Plains Missionary Baptist Church. Pastor Hill looked young, no more than thirty-five or forty years old, with a pleasant manner. His short height and slim build gave him a boyish look, but his beard aged him. He shook Chris's hand and then hugged him as if Chris was his long-lost friend.

"Do you know Reverend Perry Peyton from Bethany Baptist Church in The Bronx?" Chris asked as he loosened his grip. Bethany was his mother's church. Rev. Peyton had been pastor of the church for over twenty-five years. Most pastors knew him. Chris hadn't been to church in a long time and didn't like it anymore. His mom had forced him to attend church when he was younger, but when he finally went off to college, he was glad to escape the demands of worship, the phoniness, and the politics that made church combative rather than a righteous community.

The reason he never went home on the weekends was that his mother demanded that anyone who stayed in her house had to go to church. During the summers, Chris went to summer school and either stayed at Nina's house or rented a studio until the fall semester began. Although he kept the faith, Chris had long since left that church.

"Yes, I know Reverend Dr. Peyton. He is a good friend of my pastor, Reverend Dr. James Sensor of Corinth Baptist Church in Brooklyn. He is truly a great preacher. Why, is he your pastor?" Reverend Hill asked. Chris told him it was the family church, then skirted the issue and asked him to do the opening prayer when their session began. The reverend graciously agreed.

"With all due respect, Reverend," Chris began carefully, "since we're on a time limit, it'll have to be brief and to the point." He knew well that preachers tended to be long-winded.

Pastor Hill said, "I got you, young man."

The hour was fast approaching. The 2:00 p.m. show had started about five minutes late, and the lawn was packed. Barricades had to be put up on every side to prevent more cars from coming on campus. The only ones allowed in now were the bands; even some of the media had to be turned away. A police escort was used to route the bands around the traffic at the school, though Public Enemy had still not arrived. They were known for being late, but they only had less than an hour, so Chris hoped they would be on schedule. He didn't panic because Wannabe was keeping in touch with his uncle, who was keeping in touch with Public Enemy's management. Wannabe's uncle, as well as the management team, were expected to be at the show. By 2:30 p.m., they got word that they were *en route*, which was a good sign.

Chris told Sheila to bring out the dancers and choir so that they could immediately take the stage as soon as the current act ended. The performers said a prayer out back and came together as a group to stand behind the stage. Sheila was surprised at the large crowd, and so were the other guests invited by the BSU. They hadn't had time to check out the other acts because they were too busy rehearsing. Sheila went over the choreography and staging, and the dancers and choir were informed their performances had to begin and end on time. Public Enemy needed time to do their thing. Nina checked on all the volunteers and returned to assure Chris they were suited up and ready to participate. Each volunteer wore the T-shirt as a sign of solidarity, and as soon as their group ended, they would all meet near the stage.

Chris's heart was pumping as the moment of truth approached. He was impatient, compulsive, and couldn't stop asking Barry and DJ, "Where is the band?"

"They're coming." They replied each time. Chris kept telling Nina and Sheila to make sure the groups were ready to go up on stage immediately upon the other group's departure. He repeated it six times before Nina became annoyed and told him to shut up.

It was now 3:00 p.m, and the departing group used five extra minutes to wrap up and sing right up to the last minute, which they could do since they hadn't come on until five minutes after two. Before they could get off the stage, Chris led his team on.

"Hello, Quad Jam!" Chris yelled out to the crowd. They yelled back, "Public Enemy number one!" The microphone was low, so he told the sound people to turn it up. When he looked over, Jerry and his crew stood beside the sound guy. They had hired a team to do the sound and lights. They were cooperative and turned it up immediately.

Chris introduced the lineup the BSU had arranged. "We have the White Plains Baptist Church Choir, followed by the Harlem African Dancers, and last but not least, none other than PUBLIC ENEMY NUMBER ONE!" At that, the crowd went wild. Chris didn't waste any more time. He introduced Reverend Hill to open with prayer.

"Welcome, Quad Jam. I'm Reverend Hill of the White Plains Baptist Church, and I'm here . . ."

Chris nudged him. "Get on with the prayer." This was no time to get Hollywood, especially for preachers. The Reverend quickly cleared his throat, got back on course, and said a thirty-second prayer while Chris held his hand and bowed his head.

The choir immediately began to sing. They all looked beautiful in their robes. The director was very energetic. He swayed and moved the choir with a flick of a wrist while they all moved in unison. At one point, they did the electric slide, and the crowd went wild. Their voices were strong and reverberated all over the campus. Chris could see Nina smiling widely. The choir took precisely seven minutes to do their thing, and the African Dancers immediately followed them. At 3:15, Chris looked around for David, who was nowhere to be found.

"Where the hell is Wannabe?" he asked Barry

He shrugged, frowning, "No idea."

That's when Chris began to panic.

The African dancers energized the crowd even more. The drummers paved the way for the dancers to come on stage. Twenty or so dancers strode out before the crowd, led by Sheila. They were dressed in African attire with bare feet. Their choreography was perfect, and the crowd loved them.

Chris told Barry to stay where he was and work the crowd if he wasn't back in five minutes. The dance was supposed to end at 3:25, which provided enough time to introduce Public Enemy and allow them to do their act for half an hour.

Chris went in search of Wannabe but didn't see him. His pulse raced and sweat coated his skin. By the time he reached the parking lot, it felt as if Chris had looked everywhere, and still, there was no sign of Public Enemy. He ran back toward the stage but getting through the crowd from the parking lot was crazy. Chris looked at his watch. It was 3:25. He could hear Barry on stage revving up the crowd from a distance. "Are you ready for Public Enemy number one?" Barry yelled. Chris was relieved. Barry thought to kill time by rapping for a while, which held the crowd's attention for a little longer. He felt sick to his stomach. What if they didn't show up?

Just when he was about to turn and search for Wannabe again, Public Enemy came on stage to the opening strains of their hit song: "Public Enemy number one. One, one, one, one." He ran back towards the stage as the crowd went wild. Chuck D and Flavor Flav sang "Fight the Power," and the crowd sang along. The band sang four songs in thirty minutes, all of which the crowd sang and danced to. They brought the whole crew, including the DJ and S1W security. Chris got a chance to meet

Wannabe's uncle and spoke to the management team while Public Enemy was performing. They commended him for a job well done and said they would keep in touch because they wanted Public Enemy to do more college events. They ended with their new song, "Bring Da Noise," which was already a megahit.

As they left the stage, they publicly thanked the BSU, Chris, Barry, DJ, Nina, Sheila, and David for inviting them. Flavor Flav said, "Yeahhhhh, boyyyy," and as quickly as they came, they left.

The BSU had three minutes left to their hour, and Chris used the opportunity to get up in front of the mic and reiterate their demands to the administration. He pulled out his list and asked all Black Student Union supporters to come on stage quickly. Nina led the way and stood next to him. They had already given stage passes to those who helped coordinate the event. Some people began to boo them for getting political. But as student union members came up, Chris started to read anyway. The booing got even louder.

"We want more African American Faculty. We want an African American Studies Department. We want more…"

Suddenly the sound cut out. Chris checked his watch, and they still had one minute and twenty seconds. He yelled out, "Put the sound back on." All he could see was Jerry waving his hand and saying, "Your time is up." Chris yelled back, "We still have one minute." The crowd began to boo again. This time, he didn't know if it was against them or against Jerry and his cohorts for cutting off the sound.

Barry started cussing at Jerry.

"You better put the sound back on before I come down there and kick your ass!" Chris calmed him down, but everyone on stage was wondering what to do next.

"What do you want us to do?" Nina asked. Chris told Nina to make sure all the coordinators stayed on stage. She went to the end of the line and stayed by them. Some in the crowd started yelling, "Get off the stage," while others shouted, "Put the sound back on."

"Hell no," Chris roared. "We ain't going nowhere!" They were entitled to one full hour. It was still their stage time, and they were being disrespected. Chris turned around and raised his arms to get everyone's attention, then told all those standing on the stage with him, "We ain't leaving." They were with him and began to shout, "Fight the power. We've got to fight the powers that be." They were hyped because of Public Enemy. Chris told everyone to sit, and they sat on the stage as one without any intention of moving.

The crowd was now visibly upset while the security guards just stood in front of the stage. They were not the police; they were just there to protect the acts and keep people from getting near the stage. They didn't know what to do when things started to go downhill. The event went from jovial and united to angry and divided in three minutes. It's true what they say, music unites, but the absence of music causes hell.

More booing ensued, and some people from the crowd started throwing beer cans. Barry got upset and was about to jump down from the stage into the crowd, but Chris pulled him up short.

"Just sit tight."

Barry glowered first at the crowd and then at him. "I ain't into that MLK nonviolent stuff. If one of those cans hit me, I'm kicking ass."

Chris told Nina to go behind the coordinators. He didn't want her getting hit because he would lose it if she did. She quickly complied.

It got ugly when guys in the crowd burst through the security line, ran up to the stage, and tried to pull some White volunteers off the stage. Some turned on Chris and Barry, who were more than ready to defend themselves. Chris's knuckles grew sore with all the White faces he struck. A part of him enjoyed every moment until he saw the police rushing through the crowd toward the stage, pushing and shoving people out the way. Everything looked chaotic from where he was standing. The singing and dancing had turned into screaming and fist fighting. White guys were fighting White guys, and Black guys were fighting White guys, and the White girls and Black girls were fighting each other.

It was total chaos.

Even though Chris was sure they had enjoyed the show, it seemed like they were not averse to violence in its wake. For many White students, this was like a bar brawl they were very familiar with. Chris told those around him to sit there as the police approached them. The stage shook even more as lights fell. The cops began to pull people off one by one and throw them to the floor and up against the stage. They were aggressive and heavy-handed as they restrained the students with white plastic ties.

Chris was dragged away by police officers and thrown onto the ground; Barry and Wannabe received similar treatment. He felt like resisting at the injustice of it all. But then he looked over and saw DJ fighting with Tommy. DJ was whipping his ass. As they were being carted away, they kept yelling, "Fight the power! Fight the power!"

Chris had been glancing around in search of Nina and finally saw her against the stage being patted down by one of the cops. To Chris's dismay and anger, he saw the cop touch her around her chest and pat her several times on her butt. Just then, Nina turned around and punched the cop in the face, throwing him back. He then grabbed her and tossed her to the ground. Chris's heart began to beat rapidly, and his mind wandered back to the car on the day his cousin was shot. He saw blood on his hands. He felt the weight of the policeman on top of his body, holding him down, preventing him from getting to the ambulance.

Everything turned red, and Chris used all his strength to push the cop off him. He ran as fast as he could toward Nina, but before getting to her, Chris was tackled by two police officers, who held him down, pushing his face to the ground. He saw his cousin Damon, then, as his vision cleared, he saw Nina being manhandled by the police officer.

Chris fought and yelled, dirt and grass in his mouth. "Leave her alone!" Fortunately, a White female officer came to Nina's aid, put her in handcuffs, and took her to the police car. They picked Chris up and threw him in a van.

Dean Martin got on the microphone, which they had turned back on during the chaos, and told everyone to calm down. He begged and pleaded, but no one listened. The police van came, and about fifty people were arrested, both from the BSU and the broader campus.

# CHAPTER TWELVE

Nina sat at a desk, handcuffed, and separated from the other students who were arrested. She had been taken to a room and brought to a desk where she was questioned.

"You know, out of them all, you can be in a lot of trouble." The female officer who had arrested Nina stated as she continued filing a police report.

Nina barely registered the officer's words. Nina was too upset by the injustice of what had happened to her to be frightened by the officer's threat. Her T-shirt was slightly ripped at the arm, and her jeans were full of grass and dust from being thrown on the ground.

"Why is that?" Nina asked with a fierce attitude. "The officer that touched me inappropriately should be in a lot of trouble. Why isn't he being booked? Us women must stick together." She expected the officer to take her side.

The officer looked up from her report at Nina. "Ms. Simmons, it was a routine pat down, as is customary when an officer is arresting someone."

"No, Officer…" Nina looked over to see the name on her badge. "…Grassle. It was intentional. None of the other students were patted down like that. He turned me around and touched my breast several times and patted me down and squeezed my bottom as he patted me; that's when I reacted. It was a normal reaction. I should press charges." Nina looked out the door, wondering if that cop was out there now, filling out his own paperwork.

"Well, speaking of charges, let's just hope the officer doesn't pursue additional charges against you. It's a serious offense to assault an officer and resist arrest." The words 'additional charges' struck Nina.

Nina asked the woman directly, "Officer Grassle, you're a woman. Have you ever been sexually harassed before?" Nina waited for a response, but when Officer Grassle didn't answer, Nina continued. "If you have, you would know what sexual harassment is. You know, when someone touches your body without your permission, it makes you feel uncomfortable. He used the arrest to touch me intentionally, in a wrong and nasty way, and he should be held accountable." Nina's voice shook. Officer Grassle looked up from the paperwork regarding Nina, almost with pity.

"Ms. Simmons, this is not about me. This is about you and whether what you did – punching a police officer while performing his duties – will be considered a major offense or will be dropped because of all the other stuff that was going on.

*Free Nina: The College Years*

I understand you're hurt, but If I were you, I would be thinking of how to get out of all this mess and hoping that the officer drops the charges." Nina watched as she wrote up the report, feeling a little scared and worried at this point. She wondered where Chris and the rest of the crew were.

---

Chris and the others found themselves in a large room in a local precinct. Since the group was so large, the cops had to put them in the jail's basement with guards at the door. The precinct couldn't accommodate all the detainees. The room they were being held in was half the size of the school cafeteria, with chairs scattered around that many kids picked up and sat on. Just as in the lunchroom on campus, most of the White kids stayed on their side, and the Black kids and a few of the most liberal White kids stayed on the other side. Barry, Wannabe, and Chris had been arrested, along with Sheila, Reverend Hill, and Sheila's dance instructor, Ms. Shepherd.

DJ had somehow escaped arrest, along with others from the BSU. On the other hand, Chris was surprised to find Jerry and Tommy there. A few of their cronies from the Student Government were also in the basement. All in all, about forty people from the stage and a handful of students from the crowd were arrested. A huge disparity. They'd arrested most protestors and allowed the rioters to go free. The T-shirts had worked to the BSU's disadvantage during the protest. The majority of those arrested were wearing the "BSU/FIGHT THE POWER" T-shirts DJ had made. The police were able to target everyone with the same T-shirt and arrest them. They called it "Black T-shirt profiling."

Out of all the familiar faces, Nina's was not included. They'd taken her straight to the precinct after arresting her for assaulting a police officer.

Chris tried to get the guard's attention for what was probably the dozenth time.

He shouted, "Hey! In case you forgot, you can't hold us here unless we're being charged with something." Someone from Jerry's group joined in the protest. Since common sense wasn't working, Chris tried a different approach. "Where's our phone call?" he demanded, "We're entitled to at least one." The guard continued to ignore them.

Barry looked as if he were about to snap. Before he could, though, Dean Martin and the college president appeared as the door opened. They looked upset. The president was a woman by the name of Marsha Save. She was very masculine-looking, with a hunchback and gray hair. She had been with the college for over twenty years as president and was a woman who didn't say much. What little she did say usually made an impact.

Everyone approached her as she entered the room, like puppies awaiting food. She looked at each of them, lips tight with disappointment. "You all should be proud and ashamed of yourselves. Proud that you were able to put on such a great event and ashamed that you had to ruin it." She spoke with poetry and passion, the sound of her voice melodious despite her tight lips. "It is a shame that we had to conclude today's event on a sour note." She continued, pronouncing each syllable with pointed precision. "Something that once brought unending praise and glory to our campus today brings shame and questions of racism and race relations." Several students ducked their heads.

"Don't worry. I am not blaming only you." She looked at each of them in turn. "We are *all* responsible for today's eruption. This has been a long time coming, unfortunately. The ravages of racism and the absence of dialogue have been brewing for a long time, and it is only now that we find ourselves confronting it." She sighed, her posture easing somewhat. "I, too, take responsibility for this rift in race relations. I want all of you to go back to school. Upon our arrival, we will discuss and hopefully find a solution to all of this. As for the charges against you, they have been dropped. You will not be booked, nor will you have an arrest record."

Chris's body sagged with relief, and he could tell that the others felt the same. Even though he didn't do anything to provoke the incident and would have fought charges tooth and nail, even the threat of an arrest record could tarnish his reputation. None of them could afford to have that kind of strike against them, especially if they planned on going to graduate school.

"What about Nina?" Chris called, catching the President's attention.

"Nina will be fine," she assured him. "Her situation just requires more paperwork." President Save checked her wristwatch. "You all will be released in a few minutes. However, the rest of the bands have been canceled, and we will not have a make-up date for Quad Jam this year."

Jerry made a sound in the back of his throat, anger contorting his face. Despite his irritation, he said nothing. His brother's band would not get to perform and close out the show the way he had hoped. His goal, Chris knew, was for them to rival Public Enemy as the best performance at the Quad Jam.

"I ask that none of you speak to the media or anyone else about this until we get a chance to fully understand what went wrong," the president said. "Any premature discussion will only exacerbate tensions and bring unnecessary attention to our campus. Many of you are graduating this year, and we want to ensure that still happens for you." Chris didn't know if that was a threat, but he agreed with her position.

"There will be vans to take you back to campus once you leave here. We're asking that you go straight to the vans, and we will meet tomorrow at noon in the Castle. Thank you for your cooperation." President Save walked out with two police officers flanking her. If her arrival had been anything like theirs, she was currently being hounded by the media and would need the buffer.

Dean Martin pulled Chris to the side as he walked out of the cell, "All you say is 'No comment at this time' and keep it moving," he said.

Chris nodded, not understanding what he was talking about.

There was still a lot to work out, but he was happy there were no charges against them and that Nina would be fine. When they walked out of the jailhouse, Chris was shocked. It had been bad before, but it was even worse now. Before they could even open the door, the media swarmed around like bees. They rushed Chris especially, seemingly aware that he was president of the BSU.

"Mr. Raine, can you tell us what happened at the campus and why you saw a need to disrupt the Quad Jam?"

"Mr. Raine, are there real racial tensions on the campus that are not being discussed? Do you believe the rap group's presence caused the violence?"

"Can you give a quick comment about how African American students are being ignored at the school?"

The reporters were bombarding him with questions from all sides. Before Chris could say, "No comment," two police officers escorted him straight to the van. When they climbed in, news of the event was all on the radio giving false information:

"Manhattanville College in Purchase, New York, erupts in violence after a rap concert.

"These rap groups are out of hand. To go into their own hood and do these things is one thing but to go to a prestigious campus like Manhattanville and promote violence, anti-patriotism, and Black power is another," a radio announcer said. As usual, the media was already distorting things. Barry and Chris couldn't believe all the attention; the fight was bigger than the concert itself. Thankfully, they rode back to the campus in separate vans from Jerry and his crew.

As they pulled from the curb, Chris saw Jerry trying to speak to the media, but an officer pushed him along to the second van. After hearing the radio distortion of the event, Chris said to Barry, "Don't believe the hype." Barry loved it and Chris could tell he was hoping for an opportunity to address the press. Chris told him that it was best to stay quiet for a moment. After all, the school had gotten them out of jail with no charges.

When they returned to campus, the media was also at the school gate; however, heavy security kept them from getting on campus. Chris saw all the major news networks were represented. With all the attention, you'd think they were covering a murder. They took pictures as the van Chris was in drove through the gate. Barry and Sheila waved at the cameras while Chris sat there, concerned about Nina and hoping everything would work out as smoothly as the president claimed.

## CHAPTER THIRTEEN

By the time they returned to campus, it was 8:00 p.m. The school was dark, and a solemn gloom hung over it. There was not even a star in the sky. The quad was empty; beer cans and trash and big patches of dirt were all over the once-groomed grass. The legs that held the stage had snapped, leaving the once-grand stage looking like a dead whale that had washed up on shore. The pillar that held up the screen was torn down, and all but one of the spotlights were blown out and hanging on the ground. Even the barricades had been knocked over. For the first time in Chris's four years, the campus looked like the hood he had grown up in, with no care, no love, and no attention shown to it.

DJ ran up to the van as it came to a stop and asked if everyone was okay. He had a wrap around his hand, Chris guessed from the fight with Tommy.

"Where were *you*?" Barry demanded.

"Yeah," Sheila grumbled, "your ass should have been in there with us."

"What?" DJ flushed with embarrassment.

The exchange reminded Chris of a conversation he read between two writers, Ralph Waldo Emerson and his friend Henry David Thoreau. Thoreau denounced the Mexican American War by refusing to pay his taxes, so he was put in jail. Emerson visited Thoreau in jail one day and asked, "What are you doing in there?" Thoreau replied, "What are you doing out there?"

DJ told them the officers restrained him but that he'd broken loose and gotten away. He only found out later that they all had gotten arrested. But this was no time to make anybody feel guilty about not getting arrested. DJ was a hard worker and a great supporter, so Chris defended him.

"We needed him here. There always has to be someone to stay back just in case we need bail. During presidential speeches to the nation and Congress, one cabinet member must stay behind just in case of an emergency. DJ was the ace up our sleeves." They all agreed about that. "Plus," Chris continued, "I saw DJ giving Tommy an old-fashioned ass whipping." Everyone laughed, and Barry patted DJ on his back.

"And besides," DJ added with a look of confrontation. "If we were in the hood or enslaved, you wouldn't get mad at the one who got away from the Five-O or enslaver. You get mad at the one who got caught by them." DJ asserted

"Ok, we get it." Barry and Sheila said, mostly to shut him up.

They all walked backed to Chris's room while DJ told them that the protests and arrests were all over the news, and they looked like stars.

In the room, they turned on the television, and there was footage of Barry and Chris being arrested. Barry was kicking and screaming, and the officers were carrying Chris because he wouldn't stand. Wannabe was fighting with one of the police officers, but they didn't arrest him for assaulting a police officer like they had Nina. The video showed the protestors sitting on the stage and the crowd going crazy.

Although most of the White guys and girls in the crowd were acting unruly and fighting, the media painted the Black Student Union as troublemakers and rabble-rousers. They focused on the Black students resisting arrest, and commentary was about the students creating a riot at an event that was normally a point of pride for the school. They kept insinuating that Public Enemy had caused racial tensions on the campus and encouraged the violence that took place, even going so far as to refer to the lyrics as violent. The media was biased in its presentation, and Chris had a feeling the BSU would have to clarify what had really happened, regardless of what the president said about letting the story blow over.

One good thing was that the school couldn't stop Reverend Hill or Ms. Shepherd from speaking to the media. They were able to give the real story and defend the BSU and the protestors who were arrested as victims rather than disruptors. Reverend

Hill especially seemed to love the limelight. Every time Chris turned the channel, he was talking to a different reporter. Chris knew that pastors loved attention, and while it would normally annoy him, it worked for him this time.

It was getting late, and Chris wanted to know what had happened to Nina. He told the guys they might have to go down to the precinct to get her, which meant evading the police officers and media to get off-campus. They were ready to go, but someone knocked on the door before they could leave. It was Nina. Chris almost cried. She had a small gash on her face from being thrown to the floor by the officer, but she looked happy when she walked in. Everyone gathered around her and hugged her. Impatient to make sure that she was all right, Chris shoved everyone else aside so that he could gather her into his arms.

Holding her, he lifted her. "You were supposed to fight the power, not the police," he said laughingly.

Barry blurted out, "Fuck tha police!" Everybody had witnessed the punch Nina landed on the policeman, and they laughed as well. For Nina, hitting a police officer was out of character. Although Nina could be confrontational and loud at times, it was only with people she knew, like Barry. She would also punch Chris playfully, but Nina always chose common sense over violence. But everyone has their limits, Chris thought, and Nina was no different.

"Bamm is all I saw, girl," Sheila chuckled. "We should call you Nina-Ali from now on." Again, the room was filled with laughter.

Barry looked at Nina and snorted, "I ain't messing with you no more," he teased. "You can keep talking that womanist stuff all you want. I'm not about to get knocked out by no woman." After everything that had gone down, turning a bad situation into a funny one felt good.

"He touched me. I should press charges against that bum and sue the police department for sexual harassment," Nina said, still angry.

She explained that President Save and Dean Martin spoke to the police sergeant. After a year, he'd agreed to erase the information from the police record. They didn't actually charge her, but the arrest information would be in the system for one year. The president also told Nina not to speak to the media about the deal, or it would create additional problems for the school and the police department. Nina reluctantly agreed though she had doubts about not speaking to the media. The media had been waiting for her when she'd walked out of the precinct. It was tempting to get her story out there.

"Yeah, the press has been calling all of us." Barry admitted, "But we promised we wouldn't speak yet." Chris thought about allowing DJ to speak since he wasn't part of the deal, but he had a problem joking too much and might say something that would hurt rather than help. Instead, he told the crew that the school couldn't silence them forever. First, they would wait to see what the administration planned and then determine how to deal with the media afterward.

In the meantime, Chris had to prepare for a meeting with the president tomorrow at noon. He told everyone they could turn these lemons into lemonade. As president of the BSU, he needed to make sure that the school met all their demands before graduation. They would bring the terms to the table and insist on them being implemented immediately. Everyone agreed to meet in the cafeteria at 11:30 am to go to the meeting together.

Chris stayed with Nina. She was worried about her grandmother since she hadn't spoken to her all day. He had forgotten about the elderly woman with all the commotion and said she should call immediately. Nina explained that she had tried, but no one had picked up. She tried again just to be sure, and there was still no answer. Next, Nina called her grandmother's neighbor, Ms. Rodriguez, who usually looked out for the older woman when Nina was away. The neighbor said she would go next door and check on Nina's grandmother.

When she called back a couple of minutes later, she reported that Nina's grandmother was fine. Chris felt Nina sag in relief.

"Can you tell her to answer the phone, please?" he asked, giving Nina a moment to collect herself. They called her grandmother again, and this time she answered the phone.

"Hey, momma. How are you."

"Nina, is that you? I can't hear you that well. When are you coming to see me? I haven't seen you since last week."

"I'm coming. I just have some work to finish. Are you ok?"

"What, you sound so low. Are you ok? I feel like something is wrong with you." Her grandmother knew her, and she sensed there was a problem.

"Yes, momma, I'm ok. It was a tough day, but I'm better now that I hear your voice." Nina began to tear up a bit.

"Ok, Nina, you and Chris, be careful. Hopefully, I will see you soon. I just need a couple of things from the grocery store."

"Ok, momma, I'll take care of it. I love you, momma."

"Ok, goodbye. Love you, Nina."

Nina didn't tell her grandmother about anything that had transpired at Quad Jam, not even the arrest. Chris agreed that it was best she didn't say anything; it would only cause her grandmother to worry unnecessarily.

He asked Nina to stay for the night, but she wanted to return to her room to finish some work. As he walked her across the messy lawn, Chris could see Nina was not good.

"How are you feeling?" he asked. She was reticent, not at all like her usual confident self.

"I'm fine," Nina said, voice strained and the sheen of tears in her eyes. "It was just an unusual experience, being arrested. Being from The Bronx, I've heard people talk about jail, but that's not my life. I'm not a hood girl."

He stopped walking when she made that statement, and she looked up at him. "Yeah, Nina, but education has nothing to do with being arrested, especially if you're Black. You could be the first Black president of the United States and be arrested."

"I know, Chris, but that's not what I am saying," Nina shot back with tears in her eyes and looked at him as if he was the cop that manhandled and then arrested her. "I'm saying for *me*. I didn't work this hard and escape the hood to be thrown in jail. I can't believe that nasty-ass cop touched my breast and butt like that." Nina wiped at the tears that had fallen as she spoke. Chris held her as she raged, "I feel like I should press charges against them for sexual harassment, or they should drop the charges completely with no one-year probation or arrest record. I mean, no one else has an arrest record." She continued, eyes blazing as she turned to start walking toward her room again. "They said I would be fine if I don't get into trouble, but I don't want the police looking over my shoulder. At the very least, I should file a complaint against that police officer."

"Do you remember which one it was?" he asked solemnly, holding her hand as they walked across the dark dirty quad.

"No. But he wouldn't be hard to find. I think I saw him at the police station walking back and forth while I was in the precinct."

Though he hated to be the one to suggest it, Chris told Nina to think about what she was saying. He didn't think she should pursue filing a complaint since they'd dropped the charges against her. She would have an arrest record, which would be expunged after a year. Honestly, he didn't anticipate Nina getting into trouble with the law again anytime soon — if ever.

Chris didn't know if it would be wise to resurrect a case that would bring her more scrutiny than the police. The police officer could easily refute her claims of sexual harassment during a pat down, which was police procedure when apprehending someone. They would then charge Nina with resisting arrest and assaulting a police officer.

"Well, I don't believe you will get into any trouble, and before you know it, the year will be up, and the arrest record will be erased."

Nina looked annoyed. "But do you think it's right that I have to look over my shoulder for the next year? And he was wrong for touching my ass. Do you think he should get away with that?'

They had reached her dorm room. "Nina." Chris held her by the hand and said, "I don't think you have to worry about getting into trouble. I mean, really, when was the last time you were in trouble with the law?" She was silent, but he could see she disagreed. "What happened was an unfortunate incident and will probably never happen again." He wanted to convince her not to open a can of worms that could only hurt her, so he urged, "Honestly, Nina, I think you will be alright. And as for sexual harassment, you can always bring it up at the meeting tomorrow with the president."

She sighed. "I probably wouldn't be in this mess if I had gone home and taken care of my grandmother." Nina hugged him softly and then went into her room.

## CHAPTER FOURTEEN

"Oh my God, Nina, are you ok?" Chris heard Tracy say before the door closed. He ran back to his room to finish some schoolwork but fell asleep as soon as he hit the bed.

Tracy jumped up from her bed and embraced Nina while moving her towards her bed, where they both sat holding each other.

Nina's eyes teared up as Tracy hugged her for a long time. "I'm good." As Nina released her embrace, Tracy loosened hers slowly while pulling out a tissue and helping Nina wipe the tears from her eyes.

"Did that cop really touch your tits and ass? Did you file a report?"

Nina shook her head while still wiping her eyes. "No, they said I should consider myself lucky the cop didn't file additional charges against me for resisting arrest and assaulting a police officer."

"Oh, bullshit! Those suckers are full of it, the nasty bastards. If you want to, Nina, I will go with you to the precinct tomorrow and file charges. Don't let them get away with that shit!"

"I don't know, Tracy. They dropped the charges and said they will just keep the arrest record on file for a year, and all information from the precinct would be erased afterward."

"What! What did Chris say?"

"Well, Chris is not really saying. I think he believes we should just take the deal since they dropped everything. He can't see me getting into trouble in the next year, and truthfully neither can I," Nina said.

Tracy remained quiet for a while, then finally emitted a loud gusty breath. "Nina, I'm just saying, wrong is wrong, and I don't want to get in between you and Chris, but you need to do something."

"I know, and I think Chris will tomorrow at the meeting with the president. I'll be sure to bring up the issue."

"Oh, Nina, this is so disturbing. Those doughnut-eating, fat ass, out-of-shape pigs should not get away with touching your ass and making you feel guilty about it. Womanist, don't go for that mess." Tracy said supportively.

"I know. I just don't know what else to do?" Nina and Tracy hugged each other again.

# CHAPTER FIFTEEN

Chris got up about 6:00 a.m. that morning because he still had a paper to finish for his Monday class. As Professor Hines said, he had to balance activism with academics. Activism was taking over, and he didn't want anything holding up his graduation in three weeks. While he was at it, Chris also drafted a letter for the meeting with the dean and President Save, outlining what happened at Quad Jam from his perspective just in case the President asked. He attached it to the demands for hiring African American faculty and creating an African American Studies Department.

Nina came over to his dorm room around 9:00 a.m.

"Hey babe, great you're early. Did you finish your work?" he asked while completing his report for the president.

"It's almost done," Nina said solemnly. He looked at her again, knowing her demeanor meant something was wrong.

Chris went over to her. "What's up, Nina? Did you sleep alright? I told you, you could have stayed with me last night."

"No, not really. I can't concentrate knowing what the officer did and the deal I took." He expelled his breath in a huff of annoyance. They had already dealt with the issue of her arrest.

Patiently, he sat Nina on the bed. "Nina, let's not worry about the deal. Let's concentrate more on the meeting. You can speak about sexual harassment at the meeting today. That will give us a chance to deal with the issue in addition to the issue of Black faculty on this campus. The issue of sexual harassment may be able to get us a Black female faculty member in one of the departments. So, all is not lost."

"Ok, are you going to bring it up, or should I?" Nina said directly as she continued. "I think we need to add to our agenda specifics on a Black female faculty member and that sexual harassment by the police is unacceptable."

Chris wondered where Nina was going with this. He didn't want the agenda to be hijacked by a debate about gender and police harassment.

"Ok, let's feel it out, play it by ear. Any one of us could bring it up. But I think the issue of who they hire, whether male or female, shouldn't be discussed at this meeting. We need to make sure they agree to hire someone Black by next semester. We want them to hire someone, male or female, but I don't want to get into that now. We need someone Black."

"Chris, we always need Black, but like you said, this sexual harassment can open the doors for a Black woman as well, so we should be specific." He was annoyed that she was making this the issue. Rather than sticking to the plan, she was making it about sexual harassment and hiring a Black woman. He listened impatiently as she continued. "And Chris, if I have to live with this arrest record for a year, which I'm still not happy about." Nina paused, then continued. "I want an apology from the police department, and I think you still should try to organize the BSU and fight till this arrest record is rescinded. Even Tracy says it's unfair and insulting."

"Tracy!" He stood up, mad as hell that her name was even mentioned. "What does Tracy White ass know about unfair and insulting! What happened to you would never have happened to her. She has nothing to do with this, and you shouldn't discuss our business with her nasty self."

Nina looked at him wide-eyed, stood up, and then responded. "Chris, everybody knows about it. He touched my ass. He squeezed my breast. You're the one who should be outraged at him for treating me like that and them giving me probation with no consequences for his inappropriate behavior."

"Nina, I am outraged about it. You should know that. I'm the one that tried to run over there and protect you and got tackled by the police officers and thrown in jail. But I'm confident that you will be ok. That you will do your year and walk away. Why escalate a problem that's ultimately going to go away? You will continue with your career without an arrest record to show for it. On the other hand, we have a school that has been jerking us around for decades, making promises. This issue has not gone away, and here we have a chance to make changes."

He didn't like how Tracy influenced Nina and put stuff in her head that, at times, was in direct contrast with his goals and Nina's as a power couple. Thinking he had been too harsh and had broken all his father's rules on yelling at women, Chris sat Nina down on the bed and spoke softly. "Nina, I'm sorry, don't get me wrong, the deal they gave you is wrong, but I don't think you have anything to worry about. I will fight if you want me to and organize around it if you say so. But if we escalate it, then they escalate it, and it becomes a court issue on sexual harassment, police misconduct, and police procedure, and the issue of Black faculty and an African American Studies Department is lost, dismissed, at least until the other issues are resolved. I will be gone by then. And the new leadership will have to start the fight all over again." Nina looked away. He knew she didn't want to hear what he was saying, but Chris continued trying to get her back on track.

"Truthfully, Nina, if anything, you should be proud. Being arrested for punching a White male officer and almost knocking him to the ground is a badge of honor for the women's movement." Nina finally smiled at that. Encouraged, Chris continued. "You will have a great story to tell someday, and you will look back and laugh at it all. People will applaud you for your defense and defiance against an officer that represented the patriarchal system of oppression for Black men and women. You didn't get arrested for hood stuff, like you said yesterday. You got arrested for the movement. For the cause. For the Black men and women out there constantly being mistreated and harassed by police officers. A beautiful, strong Black woman like you took a punch at the system. So, I don't think you should worry about the deal. We should deal with the sexual harassment, the Black faculty, including Black women candidates as a possibility in all of this." He took Nina by the hand, hoping to ease her sorrow.

Her expression of bewilderment tinged with grief didn't change, but she said, "Ok, Chris. I just want us to have success at the end of the day. I'll trust you with the deal they gave me and leave it as is. I hope that you will bring it up or at least back me up with the police misconduct issue, and if we manage to get a Black professor, you will raise the issue of a Black woman."

"Nina, I got you. Let's just stick with the plan, and I'll definitely back you up." He promised as he hugged her.

She whispered to him. "I love you, Chris." Then pulled back from his embrace with a serious expression, "And if you ever yell at me again, I'm going to punch you in your throat, just as hard as I punched that police officer in his face. Got it." Nina stated with her fist at his throat. Chris buckled, "Yeah, got it."

Nina smiled then embraced him again." Chris squeezed her hard.

"I love you too, Nina, and I don't want anything coming between us," he whispered and then pulled back. "Not even Tracy."

Nina looked at him, laughing, sounding almost like she was back to her old self. "Chris, you know Tracy can't come between us. And don't go saying anything to her. She's just being a friend."

"Yeah, well, you can't trust promiscuous friends like her," he said jokingly, but she must have caught the undertone of sarcasm.

"Stop." Nina pulled back from him again. "She's been a good friend, like a sister. And I wish you would stop calling her names. She likes you, Chris, and what we're doing together. She's just looking out for me."

"Ok," Chris said as he pulled Nina back into his arms. "I won't say anything. Just keep her out of our business."

"You just can't help yourself, can you." Nina sighed. They made out for a while until it was time to go.

"I've got to run if I'm going to make it. We told the crew we would meet up in the cafeteria," he reminded her.

"I'll meet you over there. I have to get my books for tutoring after the meeting," Nina said as she ran out the door.

# CHAPTER SIXTEEN

At 11:30 a.m., the gang met in the cafeteria. Barry, DJ, and Wannabe were already eating when Chris got there. Sheila had not arrived, and Chris assumed she and Nina would be there soon. Meanwhile, he read the letter he had drafted for the meeting, along with the BSU's demands. The response was positive. Sheila arrived just as they were about to walk out of the cafeteria. She said she had peeked into the castle, and a host of administration and students were already present. They walked over to the castle. A guard was at the door to let only those who had been invited in. They gave their names, and he checked them off on his list.

Sheila was right; all the students arrested from the Black Student Union and those from the Student Government were there. Mark, Tommy, and Jerry were sitting up front, so Barry, DJ, Sheila, and Chris went to the front too. The president walked in with Dean Martin and Professor Hines and stood right in front. Dean Martin stood on her left, and Professor Hines stood to her right and slightly behind her.

Chris was surprised to see Professor Hines, who looked uneasy as if he didn't want to be at the meeting. Meanwhile, President Save looked anxious to get on with it. She had been avoiding the media, and Chris was sure the board of trustees was jumping all over her to resolve the matter quickly. This was the most and the worst publicity the school had ever received. If someone hadn't heard about the lily-white college before this, they sure as hell heard about it after the Quad Jam protest.

"Good afternoon, ladies and gentlemen," President Save began. "I want to thank you all for coming out. I think you know why we're here. Yesterday was one of the most embarrassing and shameful days in the history of our campus. I cannot begin to tell you how disheartened and disgusted I feel, and many of my colleagues feel the same." Her voice cracked with emotion. She looked primarily at Chris and his friends as she said, "As I told you yesterday, I am not blaming you for this school's history and its inability and ignorance to address race issues, student concerns, and faculty-student relations."

As she continued to speak, her eyes moved over all the students standing in front of her, Black and White. "However, I am holding you all accountable for the violence, the lack of consideration for each other and the campus, and the total disregard of authority that occurred yesterday."

Jerry interrupted her. "If I may, Ms. President. The BSU totally disregarded the time limit we all agreed to, and when we simply tried to get everything under control, they went crazy."

Barry jumped up. "*We* went crazy. What were *you* doing turning off the sound before our time was up? We had more than a minute left, and you cut us off. You're lucky we didn't go crazy or else…" Chris stopped him mid-sentence to prevent him from making threats at the meeting.

"That's right," Chris said, nodding. "And then, your people stormed the stage. We sat down to protest peacefully, and that's when the police came and violently pulled people off the stage as if we were the rioters and not the protesters. The violence came from members of the Student Government."

"No!" Jerry snapped. "We had nothing to do with the violence that took place. None of this would have happened if you had just ended your show."

"If you had just let us finish, there wouldn't have been a sit-in, which means there would never have been a riot, and none of us would even be here!" Sheila shot back while supporters of the BSU applauded.

President Save jumped in. "Stop it." She glared at all the students seemingly at the same time. "You are telling me that you were fighting over a minute? Really? You say you had a minute." She looked at Chris. "You say they didn't have a minute." She looked at Jerry. "Obviously, this is about more than time because a minute would not have mattered if you were working with each other. This is about respect. You don't respect each other as students, as leaders, as Black and White people, as liberals and conservatives. Respect would have given a minute, and respect would have given up a minute to keep the peace."

This was the president Chris had seen speak about Manhattanville College on previous occasions. She was her passionate, poetic self and was every inch the president. She had hit on the crux of the matter. The Black students did not feel respected, and Chris agreed. He had to also admit that they hadn't shown any respect for the student leaders who had dissed them either.

Just then, Nina walked in and stood next to Chris; she stared at the President as she continued to speak. "I can't tell you how disappointed I am in all of us for not seeing that there was a respect problem on this campus. All students and faculty members should respect one another enough to be able to work together regardless of color or political perspective."

"We're more diverse than them," Sheila assured her.

"Is this about *them* and *us*?" President Save asked.

"Yes!" Chris exclaimed before Sheila could answer. "When we have to scream and yell so that someone hears us. When we're constantly ignored, it becomes a battle. We finally get our day, and we're cut off, then yes, it's absolutely about them and us. We finally got what we wanted on this campus, which wasn't much. Just a music group, and yet when we finally get it, it's disrupted by inconsiderate people who can't even stick by their agreement. We ask for *one* Black faculty member and *nothing*. We beg for an African American Studies Department and *nothing*. So, we decide to fight for a spot on Quad Jam, and we get one slot out of twelve! One out of twelve! Really?" His voice rose as if he were mid-debate, thundering away at everyone in the room — including the President.

"We used what we had to the best of our ability to unite *all* the students. Black, White, Asian, and Hispanics, women, men — all working together and enjoying the day because of the one band we brought to campus. And they couldn't be a little considerate and let a minute go when they thought we'd gone over time. It's a shame, and nothing but greed, power, and disrespect would make them do such a thing. You have eleven hours every year, and you're fighting us over one minute. Ridiculous!"

"Yeah, like we some slaves," Barry blurted out to the surprise of everyone in the room.

Chris was more emotional than he had thought and was glad he didn't hold anything back. The crew applauded, and so did all those who were supporters of the BSU. Even Professor Hines had a little smile on his face like he was proud of his statement. Dean Martin looked nervous, and Jerry and his crew were silent while DJ kept clapping even after everyone had finished applauding.

President Save cleared her throat, "As I stated," she began, trying to regain control of the conversation. "A division has existed for years. I want to know what we can do to begin the healing process. How can we bring you together? How can we fix this?"

"Excuse me, President Save, I know they think we're a bunch of disrespectful, greedy, power-hungry racists that want to control everything, but they—I mean, that's not true." Mark jumped in. "I have tried to work with Chris and Sheila and the BSU. I have called them to meetings, but they have ignored us. What can you do but move on when someone ignores you? I want to work with them. I want them to be us and us to be them. They would have had six spots if they had worked with the Quad Jam Committee from the beginning. We weren't keeping the spots from them, we were organizing the event, and time was of the essence, so we had to fill the slots we had."

"Again, Mark, not true." Chris jumped in before Barry and Sheila could answer. "We have never been called to meetings, and on our part, we never inquired about them because we were never invited to them since I've been president of the BSU. We only heard about the secret meeting that was being held in the basement, and we crashed it. And if we hadn't demanded a spot, we would not have had one.

"But President Save, let me be the bigger person and not go back to pointing fingers." Chris quickly shifted the conversation and focused his attention on the president before Mark and his crew could answer. "We've made our case. For us, this was more than about a band or a minute when we were silenced. This was about an institution that has ostracized us and made empty promises to us for years. Yeah, we could have gone to the meetings and fought harder for more slots at Quad Jam, but then we would still have been playing the same old tune. Even if we were given six slots, would that have changed the make-up of this college? Would that have made a big difference to the racial disparity in the faculty? Would that have given us a Black man or woman tenure track professor?" Chris looked at Nina as he made that last statement, and she smiled. He challenged President Save and all the White faculty arrayed with her.

"The history of racism, alienation, and exclusion on this campus is well known to all of you. It is obvious. From its inception, the Quad Jam has been so flawed that in the past, the Black Student Union went ahead and planned their own celebration for the Black students in another part of the campus; like the history of J'ouvert, where enslaved Caribbeans broke away from the French carnival and had their own celebration that incorporated their own rituals. This year, we had an opportunity to get involved and thought it might be possible not only to pick a band but to stand up for our rights as students on this campus. All we wanted was for our voices to be heard, and it was a successful and sincere effort until we were cut off. We will never move forward if we stay at the back of the bus. All I can say is that if Mark, Jerry, and Tommy want to work with us, we want to work with them. Instead of it being 'us' vs. 'them,' it will be '*we*.'"

"Yes. I want to move forward as well," Mark stated.

"How many of you want to move forward?" President Save asked. Everyone raised their hand. "Good. Now, does anyone have any suggestions on how to go about doing so?" President Save inquired.

Mark was the first to speak, "Well, I think we should begin by creating a Diversity Committee that assures that the different groups are united and represented under one umbrella, rather than in so many different organizations. We need a meeting of the minds and working relations when planning events on campus so that everyone is represented."

"Thank you, Mark," President Save responded as her secretary took notes. "We have been working for some time on binding the different cultures on campus. My office will hire a Director of Multicultural Affairs who will be the liaison between the students of various organizations and cultures for the administration. The position should be filled by next semester."

She turned to Chris, and he was glad he had come prepared. "Well, we have voiced our concerns for years, maybe decades," he began. "As we just stated, nothing has been done—"

Before he could even complete the sentence, President Save jumped in. "We hired an African American tenure-track professor in the Religion Department. You were part of that interview back in February. The call went out to him this morning, and he accepted the position. He will begin in September. As for the African American Studies Department, I have asked Professor Hines to lead a committee to implement it. I am not only putting my words behind this department, I am also putting the school's money behind it. We should see something materialize by January of next year. If not, I welcome another protest led by Barry, DJ, Nina, and Sheila - who *will* be here next year as the leadership of the Black Student Union."

Chris and the whole BSU and their supporters began to applaud. DJ jumped on Barry and Chris and started screaming, "Yeah boyyyyy." Chris was surprised and pleased. He hadn't expected anything to materialize that quickly, but then again, it had been years in the making. He stood quietly smiling until Nina squeezed his hand, then he reassured her, "We'll work on getting a Black woman faculty member in the African American Studies Department." She smiled, satisfied. Barry, DJ, and Sheila were clearly ecstatic as well that their demands were finally being met.

Jerry jumped in as if to suggest that the White students hadn't received anything in the deal. "As the Student Government, we need more funding for our projects. We are often restricted when trying to give money to student organizations. Is it possible to increase the budget for each student association on campus from twenty-five hundred dollars a year to thirty-five hundred dollars a year?" It was a big demand. President Save went over to Dean Martin and spoke with him for about two minutes. She came back and said, "No. However, we can increase it to four thousand dollars a year for each student organization." Mark, Jerry, and Tommy, along with every student in the room, clapped their hands, and so did Chris and his crew. That would mean more money for the BSU next year, too.

"Is there anything else?" President Save asked. When no one said a word, she continued, "Good. Then I need you all to do something for the college." Chris had known this was coming. He had learned that in politics, everything was a deal. No one did something for nothing. Everyone had to leave the table satisfied, and compromises had to be made for that to happen. Although Lincoln was not in office at the time, he was unhappy with the Compromise of 1850 because it bolstered the Fugitive Slave Law, which allowed enslavers to recapture those enslaved who ran away to non-slave-holding States. Lincoln's devotion to the Union led him to accept the compromise so that slavery wouldn't increase in the anti-slave States and newly acquired States. Chris didn't know what she would ask them for, but he knew she hadn't met all their demands for nothing.

"None of you should speak to the media," President Save said. "I think there has been enough distortion of the events that took place at Quad Jam, and the campus has been negatively affected by the attention we have already received. School staff, including myself, have refused to speak to the press during this time. However, my office is prepared to send a press statement tomorrow, which will include the discussion we just had about African American faculty and student funding. It will state." She opened her folder and began reading from a prepared statement.

*"Manhattanville College is a great school with a rich tradition of educating students of the highest rank by engaging their interests and fostering their success after graduation. We have worked hard in the past to maintain the privacy and integrity of each student. However, like all colleges, we have our challenges. This week, many witnessed the worst of us and have attributed it to neglected race relations at the school. This could not be further from the truth. Manhattanville College has a history of addressing racial issues in a positive manner.*

*Mother Dammann, President of Manhattanville College at the time, wrote in 1938 a speech entitled "Principles Versus Prejudices," which defended the need for racial diversity when its first African American student was admitted to the school. Additionally, in 1969 when 18 African American students took over Brownson Hall in protest, demanding more African American faculty, President McCormack addressed such concerns by promising action.*

*Manhattanville College has consistently made strides in the past and currently to improve our racial makeup and race relations on campus. Our African American, Hispanic, and Asian populations have increased by 20% over the last five years, and the number is expected to increase by 30% or more in the next five years. We have worked with our African American students by placing them on committees to increase the number of African American administrators and faculty members on campus. We have successfully hired an African American tenure-track faculty member. We are also in the process of developing an African American Studies Department.*

*We have been dedicated to integrating the student body and working with all our students from various backgrounds so they can be fully represented on this campus. Also, our campus is committed to hiring a Director of Multicultural Affairs by next semester to ensure the working relations of all student organizations are under one umbrella. Our students are working together through a Diversity Committee, and with increased funding for student organizations on campus."*

She nodded toward Mark and Jerry as she read off the last sentence. Chris didn't know whether she had planned to increase funding all along or was just indicating that she'd added the last bit as she read based on their requests.

*"Manhattanville College is committed to the school's future, but more importantly, to the future of America. America is becoming increasingly diverse,*

*and as America grows, so will our commitment to campus diversity. Without compromising our rigorous standards for scholarship, we will strive to reach students of all backgrounds so that we may reflect the changing landscape of our country."*

Everyone seemed satisfied with the letter. Nina, however, nudged Chris and whispered. "She didn't say anything about the sexual harassment." Before he could answer, Nina spoke up.

"Why can't we speak to the media?" She addressed Chris, but her voice was loud enough for the others to hear.

"Well, Nina," Nina's gaze moved from Chris to President Save as she responded to the query. "There has already been a lot said. While some of it is true, most of it is not. With the many voices, it's bound to add fuel to the fire of division rather than encourage hope and unity for the future."

"Yes, but your statement doesn't clarify that neither the Black Student Union nor the band they hired was the instigator of the violence as the media has said, nor does it say anything about the misconduct of the violent police officers and – in my case – abusive of their authority. That letter clears the school but doesn't clear us."

Chris jumped in to support Nina when she glanced at him expectantly.

"I think she's right. I believe we should have a few students speak to the media, such as myself and Mark. We can prepare statements as you did. We will be cordial and fair and seek to project our future aspirations rather than rehash dissent. We will mention our willingness and ability as students to work with each other and the administration's ability to work with us to secure more faculty of color."

Nina chimed in once more. "We have to also add that the police got out of hand and, if they didn't actually cause the riot, they certainly increased tensions. They sexually harassed me, and I'm sure others. I defended myself, and they locked me up. I had to settle for a deal not to get into trouble for a year, and only then will my arrest record be erased. I think it's totally unfair." Chris was surprised Nina had brought up the stuff about her arrest and hoped that that wouldn't lead to other issues and derail the issue of Black faculty.

"No, we don't want to blame the police," Tommy fired back. "They were doing their job, and they did decide to drop the charges."

"Feeling her up is not doing their job. It's sexual harassment!" Sheila stood up and yelled out.

Nina shook her head in disgust, "Some of them were doing their job; others were being dogs. We must address this. I think it's a real problem for police officers to sexually harass females. I felt violated."

"I agree," Chris spoke up.

Nina was visibly upset, and he could see where she was coming from. Her run-in with the police officer must have been especially hard for her to stomach, given her views. Nina did not like women being disrespected. Her views were shaped by the radical women who denounced sexism and chauvinism, and racism. She went so far as to see both White and Black men as the oppressors of Black women, suggesting that Black male activists were quick to denounce racist government actions and police shootings of Black males but often overlooked and intentionally ignored issues that were important to Black women such as rape and domestic violence.

Nina was even more of a Womanist/Feminist than a Black activist. While Chris's fight was with the White political structure, her fight was with a male-dominated society. So, going after a sexist police officer who had harassed her was not just part of her fight for the cause but also a necessary action to defend her character. She could not rest peacefully unless it was addressed. Chris just didn't see the need to bring up the deal with the police station at this meeting.

"Yeah," interjected a young White kid who had been part of the protest. "A lot of those cops were out of hand. I was hit on the head with a club. I had to get stitches."

"I have an idea," President Save submitted. "Why don't Chris, Sheila, and Nina get together with Mark, Jerry, and Tommy and draft a press release. In it, you can state your positions and hopefully come to a positive conclusion about where the school is headed. Chris and Mark will be the spokespeople if the media decides to call. Before submitting it to the media, I ask that Dean Martin and myself review it." Everyone agreed, and the meeting ended on a cordial note.

Sheila, Nina, and Chris met with Mark, Jerry, and Tommy the next day. Although the president restricted it to the six of them, Chris brought DJ and Barry along. The Black students were prepared with the report Chris had drafted, and so were the others. After a lot of debate over minor disagreements, they drafted a letter together.

> *The Manhattanville College Diversity Committee would like to apologize for the uproar that took place at Quad Jam. The student body expected a good time and to enjoy the bands and were interrupted by a minor dispute that turned violent and caused the shutdown of the entire event. We also apologize to the bands who could not perform due to the disturbance.*
>
> *Unfortunately, this problem resulted from a lack of communication and working relations between faculty, students of diverse backgrounds, the administration and the authorities. There is no doubt that had the Student Government, and the Quad Jam Committee worked more closely with the Black Student Union and vice versa, the commotion*

*could have been prevented. However, we would like to clarify some misunderstandings that have been circulating in the media.*

*First, the rap group Public Enemy did not incite violence. If anything, they united the campus. The campus had never seen such a great turnout of students from diverse backgrounds working together as they did during the appearance of Public Enemy. Everyone enjoyed them, and it was not until they left the stage that things began to deteriorate.*

*Second, although we must drastically improve race relations at Manhattanville College, the misunderstanding that resulted in the uproar was not about race but rather the timing of each show. The Black Student Union, Student Government, and Quad Jam Committee take full responsibility for responding immaturely to this misunderstanding. We apologize again to anyone physically and emotionally affected by it.*

*Third, the Black Student Union was not responsible for inciting violence during Quad Jam. The BSU has had many social events in the past, none of which ended in violence. The BSU was responsible for a peaceful protest, which included students of diverse backgrounds—Black, White,*

*Asian, and Hispanic—engaging in and supporting the demonstration.*

*Fourth, we would like to thank those law enforcement officers for doing their best to control the crowd. Most of them were cordial and respectful under extremely difficult circumstances. We applaud their restraint and resolve to drop all charges against those taken into custody.*

*However, there were instances of sexual harassment and excessive force. One of our students was intentionally groped by an officer, and another was hit with a police club, which resulted in stitches to the eye. We denounce such actions and hope to improve police-campus relations in the future. We hope the police department will train their officers in emergencies like the one at Quad Jam so that all police officers will be more professional when confronted with such instances.*

*Finally, we thank President Save and the administration for working with us to address racism, increase funding to student organizations, and increase the number of faculty of color on campus. They are fully committed to implementing many of these changes before the end of the school year.*

> *Again, we apologize, and we believe Manhattanville College will be a better school because of this unfortunate incident.*
>
> Christopher Raine and Mark Jacobs, Chairs
> Diversity Committee, Manhattanville College

Everyone was happy with the letter, including Nina. Even if she couldn't file charges directly or get the arrest record dropped, at least the letter raised the issue and let the media know about the police misconduct. President Save and Dean Martin did not make a single change to the text. The president's letter went out on Monday, and the student's statement was released on Tuesday.

The next couple of weeks were crazy, constantly fielding questions from the media. Chris and the others were invited for interviews on several national and local television programs and radio shows. Chris always wore the shirt that DJ had made to the interviews. The story had become huge news and shone a light on campuses all over the nation dealing with racism, a lack of Black faculty, and police misconduct. Sometimes Mark and Chris appeared together, other times separately. The good thing is that both stuck to the script. When they appeared together on shows, they were cordial, even during disagreements. Chris was invited to speak at other colleges facing the same challenges of race. His high school in The Bronx asked him to be the keynote speaker at graduation that year.

The police station even sent a letter of apology for any misconduct by their police officers, and the sergeant personally came to the campus. He wanted to know how they could better prepare for future events. Nina challenged the police officers to develop a sexual harassment workshop to prevent incidents like hers from re-occurring. Although they said yes, there was no way to know if they pursued it. Nina still wanted to have them erase the arrest record against her immediately, rather than waiting the year, but Chris told her not to worry about it. They had done enough to deal with the issue of police misconduct. They had won the argument. He told her there was no reason to think she would get into more trouble, so what was the point? Nina finally agreed.

After a while, the media calmed down, and the hubbub finally faded. The national media was quickly diverted from the aftermath of Quad Jam by an incident involving footage of riots that were occurring because of the acquittal of four White police officers for beating a Black man named Rodney King unmercifully.

Finally, Chris was able to get back to concentrating on his studies. Through it all, he had to prepare for finals. The stress was all worth it when Professor Hines informed him that he would graduate with honors. Chris and Nina were thrilled by the news.

# CHAPTER SEVENTEEN

Chris decided to throw a party in his suite the night before graduation. Although his room was small, the suite had a nice size living room that held about thirteen people uncomfortably. They dimmed the lights and blasted LL Cool J's "Momma Said Knock You Out." Everyone contributed food and drinks.

There was a lot to celebrate.

Barry was the most excited. "I got an internship with Public Enemy for the summer! I'm the next big thing in Hip Hop Y'all! You all bow down to Barry-Tone, on the microphone, all the ladies in the place won't leave me alone!" Barry hollered out with a microphone in one hand and beer in the other. He was ecstatic and could hardly contain himself.

DJ was getting rich off his T-shirts. "I'm the next rich ass because I'll be making all the gear for Barry and every other Hip-Hop entertainer out there. I'm the King!" DJ yelled out with a shirt in one hand and a liquor bottle in the other, dancing crazily to the music playing. He was getting orders from all over the world and had even developed a couple of different shirts with his signature mark on them.

Sheila got the lead role in a show with her dance company. "Well, I'm getting closer to Broadwayyyyyy!" Sheila sang. "I'll be the lead dancer in an off-Broadway play in October! Woooooo!" She started dancing with DJ. Everybody hugged Sheila while she demanded that they all had to be there on opening night in October.

Wannabe, graduating with Chris, would be attending graduate school.

"Well, I'll still be in school while you mo-fos are getting rich and famous. I got accepted into NYU graduate school of Sociology!" Wannabe announced. Everybody gave Wannabe a big high five and congratulated him.

Despite all that she had gone through, Nina had managed to pull herself together, get past the harassment situation, and earn high scores in all her classes. She was happy about where things were going with her life.

"Well, I feel good!" Nina shouted along with everybody else. "Although I went through a lot this year, I thank God I was able to finish the year with high honors from the Psychology Department." Before she could get the next sentence out, Sheila shouted, "You go, girl!"

Everyone cheered Nina on as she continued, "Wait, wait!" Everyone quieted down. "I also got letters from the top graduate school in psychology begging me to attend next year

*Free Nina: The College Years*

when I graduate, and they would give me a full scholarship if I attended!" Everyone cheered even louder. Nina started crying even more as everyone surrounded and hugged her. It was so good to see Nina happy and smiling again.

DJ started singing along with the music. "Momma said knock you out." As they all joined in.

"Your turn Chris. You know you have some good news too, my love," Nina said, hugging him almost in a chokehold.

Everyone looked at him eagerly. "Well, I've been holding information in for over a month so that I could decide best where I would attend. I was accepted into Duke, Princeton, and Columbia law schools! I have decided to go to Columbia."

"You smart ass," Wannabe yelled out.

Barry poured the whole bottle of beer on Chris's head.

"Yeah, the other schools are too far. I want him somewhere I can get to him if I needed to, or he could get to me." Nina kissed him as the beer dripped down his face.

Everyone had a great time that night. It had been an eventful spring, and they had made it through it all. They laughed about all of it, even going to jail, Public Enemy, the face punch that Nina put on the police officer, and the media exposure. They were still marveling at how a terrible incident had led to the transformation of Manhattanville College at long last. Chris wondered if it had been necessary for them to suffer physical abuse and go to jail to see change.

They had not been born during the civil rights struggles of the 1950s and '60s, but they had gotten a taste of what it might have been like. Chris's father had given him information, but it was not until he experienced it that he felt a connection between the past and present. So many civil rights leaders and advocates of the cause had been beaten and killed; even the ones still breathing had gone to jail many times to win various rights, such as their civil rights and voting rights and all the rights they enjoyed today. Even going to a White college would have been impossible without the sacrifices and hard work of their teachers and their parents' generation. They felt connected to the historical struggle of their race and their allies in the movement.

"We made this little campus famous!" Barry hooted.

Nina's roommate, Tracy, wound up coming to the party with her new boyfriend. Henry, the undercover activist, showed up with his White girlfriend, and a couple of other girls that Barry had invited also came. DJ and Sheila got closer that night. The students danced, drank, smoked, and sang until it got late. Nina was especially happy after all that she had been through, and Chris was glad that she had seemed to come to terms with everything.

By 12:30 a.m., everybody had either left or fallen asleep in the extra bed or on the couch. Nina and Chris retired to his room. Once alone, they kissed until they were both shaking with desire. Passion stretched from their lips to their bodies. Chris stroked her tongue with his own and pulled back from the kiss only long enough to drag lips and teeth down the column of her throat.

As he devoted himself to exploring every inch of her neck, Nina said breathlessly, "I want to thank you Chris for being a good boyfriend and friend, for sticking by me and assuring me that everything was going to be alright. I believe in you, Chris, and I want us always to be together. I love you." They were both lost to the sensuality of the moment.

"I love you too so much," Chris said softly and passionately.

Nina moaned as he stroked her breast through her blouse. Unable to resist for another moment, Chris stripped off her blouse and bra and began kissing her breasts. He pulled her closer, and she moved her hands over his chest and back, breathing hard.

Chris started to unfasten her pants, and as usual, she stopped him. "Wait, Chris," she panted. She reached into her pocket and quickly pulled out a condom.

Chris stared, surprised at the package in her tiny hand. "Where did you get that?"

"Tracy has plenty of them." Nina giggled, embarrassed.

"Well, she's good for something," Chris conceded, laughing.

Nina sobered suddenly. She looked into his eyes and whispered, "I want this to be special. I want us to always be together and remember each other. I love you for who you are and what you do. I want you to always love me no matter what. I believe I'm ready to give myself to you now."

With a satisfied growl, he pulled her close and began kissing her wildly. She returned the gesture, moaning and gasping beneath his searching hands and mouth. He slid down her pants and pushed them off, pressing his lips against her stomach while she squirmed beneath him. Slowly he made his way down to her hips and stopped when he reached the apex of her thighs. She was panting, and as he hovered over her, she lifted her hips in instinctive hunger. As much as he wanted to linger, Chris had been waiting for this moment for far too long. When he finally settled between her legs, Nina was as moist as he was erect. He slipped on the condom, and once that was secure, he pressed his forehead against hers and began to gently work his way inside her.

It was slow going; he forced himself to pause each time she winced, murmuring against the shell of her ear until she relaxed again, and her excitement left her moist and ready once more. She was tight. He was persistent. When there was no more of him left to take, he began to move his hips. It took a few seconds to find the right rhythm, but soon they were moving in tandem. The passion grew, her legs tightened around his waist, and her soft cry was muffled against his shoulder. When Chris ejaculated, it was like a volcano erupting and an earthquake shaking. Nina held him tight and shook along with him. He couldn't move but simply lay still on top of her and reveled in the intimacy of losing himself within her. She whispered in his ear, holding him tight, and with a tear dripping down her eyes, she said, "I love you, Chris."

He kissed her lips gently and replied sweetly, "I love you too, Nina." Hugging her tighter, they continued, making love all through the night. They finally fell asleep in each other's arms.

# CHAPTER EIGHTEEN

May 1992

"Uhh, I'm not sure I can walk," Nina said as she slowly got up. Chris jumped up to help her as she put on her clothes.

"It's early. Where are you going?"

"I have to get back to my room and change, and you have to get ready for graduation."

"Oh yeah. I'll walk you."

"No, get ready. I'll meet you there."

"No, I'm coming," Chris said as he pulled on a shirt and jumped into a pair of pants.

They walked slowly across the lawn, Nina holding on to Chris and Chris holding Nina by her waist. They said little this time when they walked across the quad. No politics, no issues, just a sense of oddness filled the space. They made it to the dorm door, where Nina told Chris to hurry and prepare for graduation. He gave her a big hug and kiss, and she quickly entered the door and walked up the stairs. Chris quickly ran back to his room to dress for graduation.

---

"Hey, girlfriend," Tracy said, still half-sleep as Nina entered the room. She sat up and did a doubletake as she took in her friend. Fully awake at this point. "Oooh, wait a minute. Did you and Chris finally do the thang?" Tracy asked, jumping up to hug Nina as she limped towards her bed. Nina accepted her friend's one-armed hug as Tracy helped her to her bed.

Nina looked into her roommate's knowing eyes with a reluctant smile on her face. "Do you have to say it like that, Tracy? Sex is intimate and loving. If you want to know, yes. Me and Chris made love last night."

Tracy danced away from the bed, singing, "Nina's no longer a virgin, Nina's no longer a virgin.

"Stop being silly, Tracy."

"I'm not. This is big news! So how was it? Did you enjoy it? Was it good? You can tell me."

"That's too much information, Tracy. Let's just say it was memorable, and yes, I enjoyed it. It did hurt at first, but as we continued, it felt good. I'm just feeling it now." Nina turned over with legs crossed and back to Tracy.

"Oh, good! You should be happy." Tracy said, coming back to the bed to sit next to her. "You did it with the man you love, and he waited for you and popped that cherry after two-and-a-half years. You did good, girlfriend," Tracy assured her while rubbing her shoulders.

"I know, I love Chris and there are no regrets. I just sort of feel like I lost something valuable. I guess I'm wrestling with the fact that I'm no longer a virgin, which made me kinda unique with Chris. I hope he doesn't see me or treat me differently now that we had sex," Nina said, turning to face her.

Tracy shook her head. "Stop worrying, Nina. When I first did it, I was just happy to finally get it over with. I was seventeen, in a basement with a guy I had dated for three months. He was 19. It hurt really bad at first, but the more we did it, the better it felt. You're wrestling with the moral implications, the Catholic teachings."

"Yes, I did think I wanted to hold out until marriage," Nina said sadly.

"Nina, marriage is just a piece of paper. Love is what matters. People are married and don't love each other. Which one is better, to be married and not in love or to be in love and have great sex."

"Really, Tracy? The way I understand it, love, marriage, and children are supposed to add up to a happy, healthy, and heavenly life. It's more than just sex."

"Yes, that's all good stuff but this is a time to rejoice in the moment. Take time to think about the feeling, the insertion, the wetness, the heavenliness and gooooodness that come with love," Tracy stated.

"I know, I just worry a lot, but I'm good and it was good I must say." Nina grinned.

"Nina, it's with your boyfriend of two-and-a-half years. You're already unique with Chris. Don't worry. You two will be together forever. And now you can keep enjoying that D I C!"

Nina put her hands over Tracy's mouth.

"Enough," Nina commanded. "I have to get dressed for graduation, then me and Chris are going away for the summer."

"Where are you two going?" Tracy inquired.

"We're going to Orlando. Wannabe hooked us up with a timeshare his family has. And then we're going to Atlanta to visit Ed's family. I can't wait." Nina said joyfully.

"Oh, great. This is going to be the best summer you have ever had. Ain't nothing better than sunshine and sex."

"Stop it, you freak," Nina joked. "Are you going anywhere for the summer, Tracy?"

"Yeah, I'm thinking about going with Paul to Paris."

"Paul!" Nina looked at her inquisitively. "I thought Paul was old news."

"He was until he called me with tickets to Paris." They both laughed.

"Wow! Paris sounds like fun. You're right to forgive him. Well, have fun. I'm going to miss you. Thanks for being a good friend and listener. I'll call you and see you when I get back in the fall."

"No problem, girlfriend. You take care of yourself. You did good." They hugged each other, and tears filled Nina's eyes as Tracy whispered, "I'll miss you, too."

# CHAPTER NINETEEN

Graduation Day was everything Chris hoped it would be. The fresh smell of mown grass and spring flowers was in the air, and the breeze softened the sunlit sky. The laughter of families gathering to celebrate the achievements made the day even more glorious.

Graduation took place outside on the quad, which had been cleaned and groomed after the beating it took during Quad Jam. It was now restored to its former pristine appearance and glory. A white tent stood over the ceremonial stage with its podium, and before it was rows of chairs arranged on the green grass that sat at least five hundred people. The stage was graced with administration and faculty in their robes. The chairs and sidelines were filled with family and friends to witness the grand celebration. It seemed every graduate's family was in attendance, including Chris's mom. She had not been to the school since his freshman year when she and a friend had driven him to the campus.

His mother was a Bronxite and thought the suburbs too rich for her blood. She knew nothing about the school or the campus, only that her child was graduating. She attended along with a church van full of friends who accompanied her to watch him walk across the stage. The folks from the neighborhood had seen Chris on TV protesting and speaking, and many of them joined his mother in congratulating him. His mom could not have been prouder of the graduate. She smiled so hard that it was as if the grin had been painted on her face.

Chris had only been able to obtain four tickets for graduation, two of which he had given to his family, while a third had gone to Nina's grandmother. However, Nina's grandmother was too frail to attend, so all four tickets were given to his mother, so she could invite whomever she wanted. She miraculously turned the four tickets into twelve people. When she arrived, security let them through without a problem. He didn't know if her announcement that she was there to see Christopher Lee Raine graduate had eased the way. He thought security might have been afraid to deny her admittance, causing another protest on graduation day.

When Chris's name was called to come up to the stage and accept his degree, it felt like the whole campus erupted in cheers. His mom was a devoted church woman and knew how to holler. True to form, she yelled the loudest. He swore he could hear her voice from the stage. All her church folks did what Chris had dubbed 'the Black church holler,' which made the White folks look at them like they were crazy. Some of the students yelled out, 'Fight the Power. We've Got to Fight the Powers that be,' as he lifted his hand high, holding the hard-won certificate, and took a bow. The crowd erupted again for Wannabe and Mark. Chris joined in along with the other students in the Student Government and the entire Black Student Union.

It was a fitting gesture for Mark. Even though they had often been at odds during their four years attending the college, they had managed to come together to save the campus and make a difference in the end.

Nina was waiting for Chris at the end of the stage with his mother, and they each took a turn giving Chris a big kiss. His mom was a petite woman, but she was strong, and she hugged him so hard that the air left his lungs. His mom looked much younger than she was, so people often mistook her for Chris's sister, but she quickly cleared any misunderstanding. She was proud of her role as his mother, especially since she was his only family – once his father died – aside from his cousin Damon, who had virtually grown up with Chris.

Chris introduced his mother to Professor Hines, who took the opportunity to tell her what a great student he had been and advised her that he had a very promising future.

"If he stays focused, he could be the next president of the United States."

Chris's mother smiled stiffly and thanked him, but clearly, she didn't believe a word of this stranger's praises. Her expression indicated she thought Professor Hines was crazy. Chris rolled his eyes at his mother's skepticism and thanked his mentor for his many kindnesses. The professor shook Chris's hand and hugged him, whispering, "Stay balanced."

Chris looked at him and smiled, "I'll try."

His mom had reserved a table for their party at a restaurant in White Plains for a celebratory meal. Chris and Nina would meet them there. First, he had to say goodbye to Barry, DJ, and Sheila. They were waiting in the cafeteria. All of them looked as though they were going to cry, and Chris was so moved that he had to wipe his eyes. Emotions ran high among the tight-knit little group, and Chris could barely find the words to express them all.

"Stay in touch, Mr. President," Barry blurted.

"No, you're the President now, so you keep in touch," he responded.

"We just want to thank you for your leadership. I want to be just like you when I grow up," DJ stated solemnly.

"Here's your graduation gift," Sheila said, smiling impishly.

They had chipped in to get Chris a framed photo of him as the police hauled him off from his historical appearance at Quad Jam. Chuckling and staring proudly at the pic, he hugged each of them and then walked off with Nina to meet his mother.

"Don't forget about October!" Sheila yelled out. He didn't recollect what she was talking about and then remembered she was performing in a play in the city the following fall.

"I'll get there before you," he promised.

They were shown into the private room his mother had arranged for them at a nice soul food restaurant. Chris was touched by how much effort had gone into planning the celebration. The guests had already started eating the appetizers, chicken wings, and freshly baked rolls, but there was an excited buzz at Chris and Nina's arrival. He hadn't seen or spoken to the church folks in years, and it was good to see them. However, Chris was annoyed when they started asking when he would return to church. His mom knew how he felt about the church, which she had been deeply involved with since his father's death, for reasons he had never understood.

She knew he didn't like to be pressured into going to church, and she tried to save him from their demands, but she couldn't completely ward them off.

"Now that you got your degree, you should come and work with the church. Reverend Peyton would love to have you," one of the church women said while chewing on a chicken wing.

Another commented, "I heard you on television, and I heard you speak at the high school graduation. I think you have a calling to be a preacher."

"A preacher!" he repeated, disgusted, but Nina pinched him so he wouldn't say anymore that might be disrespectful to the elderly lady. But being a preacher couldn't have been further from Chris's mind. He was determined to go to law school to be a lawyer. Chris had nothing against most preachers, but he was not impressed by the profession. Aside from Martin Luther King Jr., none of them had much of a reputation for activism outside the pulpit and church. And he had found that some were hypocrites: they would preach one thing on Sunday and do another Monday through Saturday.

Even his mom's revered Reverend Peyton had been known to be slick when it came to politics and women. Although he didn't admire preachers, he did show them respect whenever he met them. A part of him also appreciated their ability to deal with Black people, who could be the most difficult in the world to lead. His uncle, on his father's side, was a pastor, and he had often told Chris's father how difficult it was to deal with church folks. Chris had plans to visit that uncle while he and Nina were traveling over the summer.

"No," Chris told the old lady he was attending law school.

She scowled, "Well excuse me. You want to be one of those Thurgood Marshall negroes. Well, good luck."

It was getting dark, and Chris told his mother they had to see Nina's grandmother before it got too late.

"How is your grandmother, Nina?" Mom asked.

"Her mind is weak, but otherwise she's physically fine. She's a trooper."

"Ok then. You be sure to tell her that I said 'hi,' and if she needs me or any of my church family to come over and bring her to church or anything, just let me know."

"Will do, Ms. Raine," Nina responded. That was one good thing about church folks; they would help anyone to church and supported the church members despite their differences.

His mother stopped him with a hand on his arm. "Oh, Chris, before you go, Ms. Hunter wants to say something to you."

Though he was anxious to get out of there, Chris knew he would never hear the end of it if he walked away from the head of the Women's Ministry at Bethany.

An older lady with gray hair and a cane stood up to speak, "Well Christopher, we are so proud of you! We, the Women's Ministry of the Bethany Baptist Church under the leadership of Reverend Dr. Perry Peyton, would like to congratulate you on your graduation and wish you success in your future endeavors. Although we have not seen you in a long time, you did grow up in Bethany. So, we all took it upon ourselves to give you a little token for your continued success." She handed him an envelope, and he hugged each of them in gratitude and gave a spirited speech of appreciation before he left.

"I thank you all, and even though you don't see me, I still know Jesus. Jesus walked with me and talked with me all through college." There were several calls of 'Amen' at that. "If it had not been for the Lord on my side, I would not be graduating."

"Preach, son!" one of the women shouted.

"I told you he gonna be a preacher." He heard one of them say to another. Chris felt it would be ungrateful not to tell them what they hoped to hear.

"I've come this far by faith, leaning on the Lord!" His voice got louder. "Trusting in his holy word. Today I stand before you and I can say church, He's never. I said never, never, never, never, failed me yet! Thank you, Jesus!"

They all clapped and shouted, 'Amen.'

Even though he hadn't been to church in a long time, Chris knew what made church folks shout. All you had to do was say 'Jesus' and accompany it with familiar sayings, "God is good," "If it had not been for the Lord on my side," "We've come this far by faith," and you had them. One thing Chris liked about church folks was that even though they could be crazy, cruel, and hypocritical at times, they could also be considerate, kind, and generous. Unfortunately, even when they were considerate and kind, it was like they were putting on a show to impress instead of doing it for Jesus. He could appreciate their kindness but couldn't be around them long.

Finally, he told everyone he had to go and would hopefully see them soon. "Thank you for the wonderful celebration and gift." They all continued enjoying the food like a Sunday afternoon dinner as he turned to go.

"Chris, I'll see you tonight," his mother said. He thought about it for a moment. It was Saturday, and she would expect him to go to church on Sunday if he spent the night at home, especially since the church members had gone out of their way to give him a gift. He would seem rude and ungrateful otherwise. Resigned to the possibility of another day of church zeal, he told her he would be home late, took Nina, and left.

Nina urged him to open the envelope as soon as they left the restaurant. It contained five hundred dollars cash with a note that said,

*God loves you.*
*Whenever you're ready,*
*we're here for you Chris.*

Chris put the card in his pocket and gave the cash to Nina, which would come in handy for their upcoming trip south. Nina and he had planned to go to Florida in July after Nina completed her mentoring program with the girls at the group home. The vacation would last throughout the summer, and they would return to the city in mid-August when school began. Because of their tight budget, they had been holding off on renting the car until the last possible minute. The money they received from the church and the money they had saved would cover their expenses and give them a little extra for the duration of their trip.

# CHAPTER TWENTY

Nina and Chris arrived at her grandmother's house at dinnertime. She was just strong enough to hobble around the house without her cane. When they arrived, she was cooking a meal for them to share. The radio played so loudly that she didn't hear them come in. When she saw them, she jumped, clutching her chest in surprise.

"You scared me, Nina."

"Well, if you would keep your hearing aid in, you would've heard us coming in the door," Nina responded, giving her grandmother a bear hug.

"Hello, Christopher. Congratulations, I hear you're the big star on campus. Nina told me you were on television. I hope you don't let all of that interfere with your graduation." Nina's grandmother was getting a little senile and had forgotten that it was graduation day.

"Mom, today was his graduation." Nina reminded her gently.

"Oh, I didn't know that. Why didn't anybody tell me? Or come and get me? I would have gone. You all don't think about me. After all I've done for both of you, you still don't think about me!" Nina comforted her, knowing there was nothing she could do to make the old woman feel better. She was moody and forgetful in her old age, and all Nina could do for her was be there.

Her grandmother had always been there for Nina, especially after her mother and father had died. Nina was only a year old when her parents took a two-week vacation to the Caribbean Islands. While flying from Bermuda to the Bahamas on a small plane, it crashed, and all ten people on board died. The Benjamins, Nina's grandmother and grandfather on her mother's side, took custody of Nina and raised her as their own. Nina kept in touch with her father's side of the family, but they weren't very close. When she was young, they sent her gifts on the holidays, but after a while, even those stopped.

Nina grew up in the South Bronx with her grandmother in a working-class housing co-op development not far from Yankee Stadium. The co-op had been purchased by Nina's grandfather and was paid off by his death five years ago. Nina's mother and father never set up a will, although they had some life insurance — which Nina's grandmother used to raise Nina and pay for her education. As a result, Nina didn't apply for the state's college tuition assistance like Chris did. Nina's grandmother received money from the state to raise Nina, and the Social Security money and Veteran's benefits from her grandfather helped pay the rest of her bills.

Nina's grandmother had very traditional values, which she impressed on Nina, and Nina held for as long as she could. Her grandmother taught her always to cover her body, especially her breasts and behind. She didn't drink and believed that smoking defiled the body. She did not believe in premarital sex until recently with Chris. Nina shared her grandmother's views, and Chris had learned that she expected him not only to conform to the old-fashioned rules but to behave with chivalry. He had to open doors for her, walk her back to her room, and any man she dated had to show his respect for her just as her grandfather had for her grandmother.

Although Nina respected her grandmother's ideals, she did not share all her talents. Grandmother found her purpose in keeping her house clean and cooking for her family, but Nina had no particular interest in emulating her in those areas. Although she kept her dorm room clean and sometimes straightened Chris's up, she didn't cook at all. They would go to the cafeteria or go out to eat. He often had to cook for her when they stayed in, which Nina loved. Like her grandmother, Nina was a strong-willed and stubborn woman at times. She had come by it naturally. Chris knew, and he loved Nina's grandmother as an extension of the woman he loved, which was why he had offered her one of his few graduation tickets before anyone else.

"Mom. We told you, and you said you didn't feel like going so we gave the ticket to Chris's mom and her friends," Nina replied.

*Free Nina: The College Years*

"Oh, just forget it." Her grandmother snapped. "See if Chris's mom will take care of you like I did." She stormed off to her room.

"Sorry, Chris, you know how she is. It'll be forgotten soon." He gave her a quick hug. Chris knew that her grandmother was a little senile. He had met her soon after he started dating Nina, and in the past two years, he found her to be a loving yet fierce personality. He even called her grandmother 'mom' like Nina did, at her insistence.

It was getting late, and instead of going back home to his mother's house and risking having to go to church the next day, Chris decided they would stay at Nina's house. Soon the perceived insult of missing his graduation was forgotten, and Nina's grandmother fed and fussed over them just as she always did. Luckily, she retired early, not thinking he and her granddaughter were crazy enough to engage in premarital sex under her roof. Chris and Nina could only be grateful, as they gave in to temptation and the hope that, along with losing her memory, grandmother was also losing her hearing.

# CHAPTER TWENTY-ONE

Chris went home late the next day because he wanted to make sure his mom had already left for church. He knew that once gone, she would be out all day. He was surprised to arrive home and find his cousin waiting. Damon was standing in the middle of the room, completely immobile, and for a moment, he reminded Chris of a photograph his mother kept on a bookshelf in her living room…a long-ago moment captured in time. When Chris saw him, Damon finally came alive. He saw Chris and grinned and swooped him up in a bear hug, making it hard for Chris to breathe.

Damon was tall and very muscular. He worked out constantly and was always looking for a quick way to make a buck on the streets rather than working for an honest living. Chris had visited him once in prison and was told not to come back. Chris guessed Damon didn't want to be seen behind bars, but Chris had at least expected to see him at graduation.

"Why didn't you come?" Chris asked, trying not to sound petulant but feeling deeply hurt.

"Man, I ain't had the right gear for that occasion, and I ain't want to embarrass you," Damon answered.

"Man, that's a weak-ass excuse. How you not going to come to your only and best cousin's graduation?"

"I know man, but to tell you the truth, I ain't into being around all those White folks. They get me nervous. And I know there was a lot of police there. You know me and the Five-O don't get along."

Chris hadn't seen much of Damon. After Damon was shot, he was arrested for an outstanding warrant and sent away. In Chris's mind, it was the best thing for Damon to keep him off the streets and from being killed. When Chris came home, Damon had recently been released and tried to keep himself straight, but Chris knew from the past that the good was no match in a battle between the thug and the good in him. No matter how much he tried to do right, wrong always won the fight. He couldn't move as well as he did before that gunshot to the stomach had almost killed him. Most of the time he stayed in the house, where he moved stiffly from one room to the other. When Chris saw Damon and how stiffly he looked, it brought back the psychological trauma of that day Damon was shot, and all Chris could do was reminisce about the good old days, when Damon was wild and crazy, to keep him from breaking down. As in the past, Damon always had something nice for Chris. Damon pulled out an envelope from the drawer and gave it to him.

"A thousand dollars!" Chris whistled. "Thanks. Where-?"

"Congratulations, man," Damon cut the question off before he could ask. "You keep fighting those mean White folks, and I'll keep fighting these mean Black streets." Damon hugged him again.

Chris cleared his throat, suddenly choked up, but covered it by asking gruffly, "Want to go get something to eat?" They had been practically inseparable since they were kids, and five minutes after seeing him again – for the first time in years – Chris couldn't remember what he'd been angry about. All he could remember was how much he liked to spend time with his cousin.

Just then, his mom came in the door. "Oh, you think you slick, negro. Coming in here after church." She took off her church hat and came at him. "You could have at least come to church to thank the Lord for allowing you to graduate. *'If it had not been for the Lord, I wouldn't have walked across that stage.'* Mom said, mimicking his performance for the church ladies the day before. "Remember the restaurant...?"

Chris laughed and backed up as she reached to grab him. "Mom, I thank God all the time, and I don't need to be in church to do it," he protested.

"Amen!" Damon shouted, feeling the spirit.

Mom ignored him and continued to glare as she trapped him behind the table, Damon helping her out and blocking the other end so Chris could not run away, just like they did when they were kids. It brought back memories for Chris, who knew Damon always stood up for his aunt.

Damon laughed, but Chris knew there was no malice in it, only amusement as they faced off. His cousin and his mom were like two peas in a pod. They had the utmost love and respect for each other. Even though they argued, and she thought that Damon should get himself together and stop his criminal behavior, she still loved him like her own. Their relationship might seem unusual to some, but they understood one another.

Chris guessed it was because his beloved cousin's mother was her favorite sister. Damon's mother, Sandra, died when he was eight; her husband Sammy shot her in the head. He only did three years in prison after claiming self-defense. Though his prison time had been cut short, Damon's father did pay for his crime. He was shot dead the same day he came home. Some attributed it to the uncles, Chris's mother's brothers, but none of them were ever investigated or charged. Sammy had too many enemies. Damon's mother was in and out of jail and drug rehabilitation for years, so Chris's mom had taken Damon in before his mother's death and raised him like her own son.

Damon and his mother shared the same outlook on life: do for yourself and those you love. Neither believed that higher education would remove a brother from the urban situation, and neither advocated activism. They weren't political, and their ambitions did not include the concept of prospering beyond their present environment. They accepted the drugs and violence in the hood as the crappy environment in The Bronx just 'was what it was.'

His mother had told him she was pleasantly surprised that she could talk to Damon about the Bible, and since he was home most of the time now, mom talked scripture and prayed often. She often prayed and cried for Damon because of his condition, and Damon said nothing, just listened. Damon didn't go to church, but in prison, he learned a lot about the Bible, so she believed he was saved from all the wrong he had done.

As for Chris, he was conflicted emotionally, theologically, and culturally. He hated the hood, but he loved Black people. The hood embodied a culture of violence, disregard for education, a poverty mentality, and a lack of motivation to escape the vile situation. At times Chris believed the church contributed to the complacency of Black people rather than the progress. Chris hated seeing Black people kill, rob, and rape Black people. He hated that God would even put Black people in such bad conditions with seemingly no way out. He hated the filth on the streets, the crime in the neighborhoods, and the lack of respect and dignity Black people had for each other.

His cousin once took him to a house where all the guys were having sex with one drunken woman. Damon thought it was funny, but Chris found it repulsive. Whenever he came home, the hood conjured up bad feelings within him. The worst had been after his cousin was shot. He took forever to recover, and it felt the hole of despair created in him by that incident would never close. His mom feared he had been permanently damaged. There was too much emotional and psychological pain associated with the place he had always called home, which is why he hardly visited his family while in school.

Chris's mom knew he had a different outlook from her own fatalism, which was why — at times — he wondered if she loved Damon more than she did him. While Damon was in prison, she visited him often. While Chris was away at college, she never came to visit. However, she called him regularly to check on his emotional and mental wellbeing. She never visited or asked him to come home. He suspected that she thought being in school in the suburbs would offer him some much-needed stability. If nothing else, he was sure she hoped it would relieve the madness that had impacted him when Damon was shot. In that, Chris believed she was looking out for his best interest. If anybody knew his history of trauma and how badly he had been emotionally and psychologically scarred, it was his mother.

He could never get her to understand why he wanted to go to that college and be around all those White people. When Chris stopped attending her church, she attributed it to his not wanting to be around *real* Black people. When she saw him on the news, she called and said, "I told you those White folks ain't no good."

Chris's motivation was clear and simple. He just wanted to get the best education the White man had to offer to bring it back to the Black community and help his people rise out of poverty, miseducation, and self-destruction. Although he went to a majority White college, he never felt comfortable surrounded by White students, faculty, and administration, so he tended to form alliances with other Black students, all from different backgrounds but all for Black people.

Chris didn't believe even Uncle Ray relished being the only person of color in a room. Most Black people move to White communities for the benefits, the safety, the chance at a better education, perhaps as a status symbol, but rarely, if ever, had he heard of anyone choosing to be the lone Black person or family in a White neighborhood or school. His mission was to bring the goods to the hood so Black people wouldn't have to move out but could stay and support their own in safety and comfort. He would love to think he could transform at least his corner of the ghettoized urban areas he had grown up in.

Even though his mom didn't understand him, she was always encouraging and prayerful. Boy, could she pray. She never came to visit him at Manhattanville, but she always sent care packages with good food, small gifts such as washcloths and soap, with notes that said, 'I love you son. Keep up the good work.'

"You should have been in church this morning," she said. "Pastor Peyton mentioned your name from the pulpit and congratulated you." He had hoped to avoid this argument, or at least put it off until much later, but she had come home early specifically to confront him, he guessed, and he was going to have to take it.

"I didn't tell him to mention my name." Chris looked at her with narrowed eyes, still trapped on one side of the table with her glaring back from the other.

"I did!" She shot a murderous look at him. "I thought you would have the decency to show up. I had to go up there and make an excuse for you." She shook her head, "You'll need the church one day. Those White folks ain't going to save you when your ass gets in trouble."

"Well as long as I have Jeeeesus, I got all I neeeeeed." He responded, goading her. She looked about to explode for a moment, recognized how ridiculous it was to argue with him, and laughed. Knowing it was safe, he came around the table so she could finally grab him, but she just sat him down and slapped him across the head as he saw Damon moving towards him and laughing.

"But you *should* go to church. They have some bad-ass girls in there," Chris heard Damon whisper. Chris's mother didn't hear him, so Chris repeated his blasphemous comment.

"Damon said I should go to church to check out the girls."

She scowled. "Shut up," she growled, aiming her ire at Damon. "Leave him alone Damon. Don't speak to him anymore. Get out of my house and go back to where you belong. In the name of Jesus, get out!"

Then she turned on Chris, "Stop listening to him. He's going to do nothing but get you into trouble. You've come too far to turn back."

"Yeah, but mom, he said your pastor be messing with the girls, too," Chris argued.

"No, I didn't," Damon shot back.

"What!" she screeched, closing her eyes in rising frustration and standing up to Damon as if she were David against Goliath. "Damon, you get the hell out of here. Don't you talk about my pastor like that." She slapped Chris over the head for listening to him, and Damon slowly ran out of the room, disappearing with a loud laugh.

Chris chuckled as his mother's gaze softened. "I'm proud of you, son." Her voice was oddly solemn suddenly. She bent down and cupped his chin in her hand, forcing him to meet her gaze. His throat tightened as he saw the tears in her eyes. "Your father would have been proud of you, too."

At that, his own eyes started to sting. Chris's father had been a good man. Older than his wife, he had loved her deeply. Even though they didn't see eye to eye on everything, she cherished him, and he loved her for who she was, a loving, supportive, caring woman and mother. His father saw beyond her faults and into her needs and showed her the utmost love and respect.

Chris's dad fought in Vietnam, came home, and went to City College, graduating with a degree in Sociology. He had been very active in the Movement and included his wife and

*Free Nina: The College Years*

young son in his activities. Chris remembered him as always reading and talking about the Black struggle and politics. He would read to his son every night, and although he didn't go to church, he read stories from the Bible and the newspapers. Chris's mother taught him how to pray, but his father taught him about the word of God in connection with the Black struggle.

As Chris got older, his father educated him about the political struggles of Black people. Chris remembered him talking about Martin Luther King Jr. and Malcolm X and how he was a member of the Black Panther Party at one time. He took his son to museums, movies, and basketball games. He loved the New York Knicks, and they would go to a game whenever he saved up a little money.

His father, however, didn't like Damon because Damon was too much of a troublemaker for him. He could not contain Damon because he would not listen and was constantly disrespectful. Once Damon was old enough to defy him outright, he didn't accept any male authority, and after that, Chris's father never took Damon anywhere.

His job as a City Planner developing homes in poor neighborhoods enabled him to move his family from the South Bronx to the Northeast Bronx into their own house when Chris was in junior high school. Although crime, drugs, and gangs existed in that working-class neighborhood, it was relatively mild compared to the projects they moved from in "the old neighborhood." Chris's father planned to return to school after ten years to get his Master's degree. He had been accepted to Hunter College, and his wife said he had been complaining of headaches for months, but like most men, when she urged him to go to the doctor, he made promises but never went. On a day visiting a site for the job, he collapsed and was rushed to the hospital by a co-worker. Unfortunately, he was pronounced dead before they got to the hospital.

Chris was thirteen years old when his father died, and the loss took its toll. He started acting up in school and hanging with his cousin Damon more often, which resulted in him getting left back in school one year. Chris would have followed his cousin's lead rather than living a life his father would have been proud of, but he sensed in his soul that despite Damon's cool façade, the banger's life wasn't a life he wanted.

Chris's mother took him to a counselor, Mr. Davis, an older Black man who reminded Chris of his father. He treated Chris almost like a son rather than a client. He helped the teenager realize that he was not only depressed but angry. He gave Chris permission to be angry at his father for leaving. If his father had been more responsible with his health and less concerned with seeming strong, he might not have died and left his young family. Deep down, Chris thought he was selfish, even though Chris didn't believe he understood that not taking care of himself would result in Dad's not being able to take care of mom and him.

But he wasn't the only one Chris was angry at; he was also mad at God for taking his father. He'd been a good dad, and Chris couldn't understand. Why, out of all the bad, no good, absent fathers, would God take his; a conscientious, hardworking Black man, devoted to his family and working for the community.

Chris had been proud of his dad. It made him feel like somebody special to have the kind of male role model that was sadly missing in so many Black families in the hood. When God took his dad, it had felt not only awful but wrong. To make matters worse, he was furious at mom's church. Because his father wasn't a member, they would not allow him to have his funeral there. That's when Chris stopped liking his mom's church and vowed as soon as he got old enough, he would never go there again. A church with a policy where membership was stronger than family was not a church he wanted to be part of. Chris never could understand why his mom remained at the church that turned his father away. When asked, she would only say, "I go to church for Jesus, not for the pastor or people."

After speaking with Mr. Davis for a year, Chris overcame his anger and was back on track. However, he had to return to him after Damon was shot because that brought back all his old feelings of betrayal, anger, and persecution that his young mind and emotions could not contain.

After he started to recover from the shooting of his cousin, Chris's focus and ambition were renewed, and all that his father taught him kicked back in with a vengeance. He went to day school and night school. He hung out at the library rather than on the streets with Damon. He was so determined to succeed that in his sophomore year in high school, the principal switched him from the probationary class with troubled students to the honors classes with promising students. Chris started hanging out with people who were just as ambitious and determined to go to college as he was. He joined the drama club and the debate team, which got him interested in law. When graduation rolled around, he had earned various awards and honors. He was confident that he would do well in college. The change in him was so extreme that the principal created a separate award called 'Student Inspiration' and asked Chris to follow the class valedictorian with an inspirational speech for the graduating class of 1988.

When his father died, he had life insurance through his job. As a result, his mom was able to pay off the mortgage on their house. However, she struggled to make ends meet when the money ran out. As a substitute teacher, she wasn't protected by the teacher's union, and she didn't qualify for the benefits given to full-time teachers.

Luckily, Chris was accepted into HEOP, the state financial assistance program that gave underprivileged students tuition to go to college. He also worked three jobs while on campus: at the bookstore, which gave him a discount on his books; the cafeteria, where he ate for free; and the gym, where he worked out during his shifts.

His mother's words about his father filled Chris with warmth. He had made it. He was a 21-year-old graduate, continuing to law school. He knew his father had hoped that he would succeed, but he didn't think he could have anticipated how well his only son would do. Even with the temptation of following Damon onto the streets and the blow of losing his father so young, he had managed to thrive. It made Chris feel good about himself. He could feel that there was truth to her words, even if the man himself wasn't here to say them.

"I know," he said, meeting her eyes. "I miss Dad all the time, but I feel him in my spirit. In my soul. I know he's here."

She hugged him for a long time as he wept on her shoulder.

# CHAPTER TWENTY-TWO

JUNE 1992

"Ok, you girls must remember to have confidence and with confidence you will value yourself and others will value your worth," Nina said as she sat around with chairs in a circle, speaking to the young women at the group home where she volunteered during the semester. Most of the girls were in their teens and high school, and they loved Nina, who spoke to them on their level.

"What do you mean by confidence." One girl asked.

"I mean where you are sure of yourself, where you know who you are and do not allow anyone to determine who you are. You are confident, sure about your worth."

"Ms. Nina, I know about confidence, but these guys don't respect confident women and so sometimes to make them feel good you have to give in," one of the young ladies responded.

"Karry, confident girls get with confident guys," Nina answered poignantly. "If he's not confident that's his problem not yours. You shouldn't have to diminish yourself, your worth, your knowledge, or your ambition because a guy doesn't feel secure in himself. Know your worth and they will either respect you or leave you alone."

"But I don't have any confidence," another girl said. "I know I'm cute and all. Guys tell me that all the time, but I don't feel smart or good about myself."

"And why not? I mean you are cute, but cute can only get you so far. You don't only want to be some guy's eye candy. Why don't you feel smart, because I've seen you walk, heard you speak and read your writing and you seem very smart to me, which should increase your confidence in yourself. You have something deeper than the surface: you have substance, a good personality, a good heart; you are more than just a pretty face," Nina shot back at the girl.

"I know but I grew up hearing just the opposite. And not having a loving family makes you feel like you're not as good as other people, not as smart, you know what I mean. I just feel like if I were as smart as you say I am, my family would love me and tell me they are proud of me. I mean, Ms. Nina, aside from you, I don't have anybody to tell me they love me, for real, not just for sex, or that they are proud of me. I feel unwanted." The girl began to tear up and Nina moved over and put her arms around her.

"Listen, Tamika, it's all good," Nina whispered, "I've been there and sometimes you just have to encourage yourself and be proud of yourself, and other people will see your love for yourself, and they'll appreciate you for you. Undoubtedly, it's hard out there, but you must love yourself so much that it produces a vibe where only loving and caring and genuine people will come your way. That's why I came your way and many of these sisters will support you as well. Sisters need to support sisters." Nina then hugged her and had everyone come and hold each other as they prayed.

"Dear heavenly Father, give these women the confidence they need and allow only the right people to come into their life. May your blessings be with them now and forever."

All the girls held up their hands and said, "Amen!"

"Listen, women, this is my last session until the fall, when I return from vacation." All the girls screeched.

"Oh, Ms. Nina, we're going to miss you. Where are you going?"

"Well, me and my boyfriend are going to Florida and then Atlanta."

"Ooooh sounds like you're going to have fun, Ms. Nina. You go, girl!" Karry said as all the girls chimed in with "oooohs."

"Well. Anyway, women," Nina said, ignoring them but smiling at the same time. "I hope you all have a wonderful summer and be careful. Keep your confidence to seal your lips and legs. There's a lot of unhealthy stuff out there, and I wouldn't want you women to catch any of it."

"Okay, Ms. Nina, thanks and we love you."

"I love you women too." They all hugged as Nina ran out.

# CHAPTER TWENTY-THREE

July 1992

It was a beautiful sunny day in July, but it was supposed to rain later that afternoon in New York, so Nina and Chris wanted to get on the road early. The rental was a brand new 1992 Ford Taurus, fully loaded. They jumped on the highway around 9:00 am and made their way to I-95 South, which would take them straight to Florida.

Chris drove. Nina pulled out the paper map and was a great navigator — when she was awake. Luckily, they weren't in a rush this time around. They made several stops then stopped in North Carolina and checked into a hotel off the highway at about 9:00 pm. It wasn't fancy, but it was clean, cheap, and had a bed. They slept, made love, and got back on the road around 11:00 am.

The air smelled different as they headed South. Nina said it was clean, but Chris said it had a calm in it. "It makes me feel like I'm just floating on clouds." She laughed but agreed. It was heavenly. They loved the smell of fresh grass, blossoming flowers, and burning wood. They could see the palm trees as they approached Florida from Savannah, Georgia — something they had not noticed the last time they were in Florida because they were in such a rush. This time they took their time and looked at the trees and smelled the fresh air. A nice departure from The Bronx and the college campus. Nina hung her head out the window and yelled: "Florida, here we come!"

When they stopped for gas, the people were amicable. Even the White Southerners were kind. One lady told Nina she looked like a movie star and Chris looked like a basketball player. They thanked her for the compliment but felt slightly insulted. Chris joked, "Yeah, they only think of us as entertainers and athletes. Never intellectuals."

Nina said, "You'll become the next Black Supreme Court Justice, and then they will."

Despite the kind words, Chris knew Southern kindness could hide racism, just as Northerners hid racism with political correctness. The Southern states had a long history of racial discrimination and outright bigotry. Not that the North was free of racial discrimination and acts of violence, but at least they were subtler about it. The South was more direct and confrontational. Chris had read about Jim Crow and all the lynchings in the South during his studies on the Civil Rights Movement.

They were careful. Nina and Chris were from the North and knew many Southern police officers and White folks felt that Northern Black people had too many privileges. They didn't want anyone to think they were arrogant and disrespectful. They feared the Southern cops wouldn't hesitate to throw them in jail for even the slightest offense.

The last time they visited Florida, Chris got pulled over by a 7-foot-tall Goliath of a White police officer for speeding. He'd been terrified. He just said 'Yes, sir' to everything *The Man* said. He didn't argue, reason, or debate him. He thanked him for the speeding ticket and told him he'd pay it as soon as he got home. He'd sensed Chris's fear, and his final words were, "If you don't pay it, I'm going to come to New York and haul your ass down here myself and throw you in jail." Then he smiled and told them to have a safe trip back home.

They arrived in Orlando at about 7:00 pm on Tuesday and checked into the suite Wannabe had reserved for them. It was beautiful. A one-bedroom with a king-size bed, a kitchen, a living room with a big television, a dining room, and a great big bathroom with a jacuzzi.

Both got in the jacuzzi naked and began their slow moves toward each other, caressing one another with deep wet kisses that rivaled the hot bubbling water in the jacuzzi. They explored different positions of sexual intimacy. Nina moaned heavily as Chris entered in and out of her. He went in deeper and moved faster and faster. Nina jerked suddenly and belted out a loud scream as she slid back and fell into the water. Chris tumbled down and fell with her. "You ok," Chris asked while holding her and laughing. She gasped as she spoke, "Oh my God, I think I had an orgasm."

Chris smiled as he held Nina and began kissing her. He pulled her back up, turned her around, and entered in from the back until he was satisfied with a loud, powerful growl that weakened him as he grabbed Nina's waist to keep from slipping. Both slid into the water with a big splash and rested on each other. They made it to the king-size bed. Nina was breathing hard, Chris lying on her, "That was so much fun." Nina whispered, thinking about the words of Tracy, 'Ain't nothing better than sunshine and sex.' Chris held her tight and whispered, "Yes it was," as they fell into a deep sleep.

The next day, Chris and Nina woke up, and he cooked them breakfast while they planned the day. Since they were going to be in the South for a month, they had to be careful with their money. Chris had about $2,000, and Nina had also brought some money. During the next couple of weeks, they got a seven-day pass to Disney and five-day access to Universal Studios. When they weren't in the theme parks, they were at nightclubs or movie theaters. The movies provided the perfect escape from the rain – which it often did in Florida. The best and most romantic times were spent in an open grass park they found not far from where they were staying or evenings on the deserted beach. They walked beside the turquoise ocean for hours or sat there looking into the azure sky, wondering about the future.

"Chris, where do you see us in ten years?" Nina asked one night as though she had read his mind.

"I see us getting our degrees, me a lawyer, you a top psychiatrist. We're making lots of money, and we own two houses, one in New York and the other in Florida for our vacations. We are married and have three children; two girls and one boy."

"Three children ten years from now!" Nina jumped up from the green grass, shattering the mellow mood. "That means I would have to start in the next three to four years."

"Yeah, what's the matter with that." He said as he pulled her back down beside him.

"Chris we're not even going to complete all our degrees by then! Well, maybe you will, but I won't, and we definitely won't be rich enough to buy two houses."

"Okay, the next fifteen years." Chris relented.

"And I'm only having two, a boy and a girl, not three," Nina said adamantly.

"I bet I'll get three out of you," Chris joked and began tickling her. She laughed so loud he had to kiss her to keep her quiet. One thing led to another, and they made love on the grass, under the stars.

To Chris, Nina was at her romantic peak during their trips; she dropped all radical Womanist talk and would tell him how much she loved him. She was affectionate and playful and just as ready as he was to engage in making love.

One day she caught him off guard when she asked, "How come you never say I love you first? Why do you always say, 'I love you, too'?"

Chris thought about her question. She was right. It was hard for him to say 'I love you' first.

Not because he didn't love Nina — he loved her with all his heart — but because he had never heard his father say it to his mom. He certainly saw his father *show* his mother love rather than tell her. He brought her flowers even when it wasn't a special day, talked to her for hours on the phone, and bought her presents, such as clothes and jewelry, just to make her feel good and special. And even though he didn't say the words, they were pretty physical, kissing and touching each other while talking.

Despite that, Chris couldn't remember hearing his father say aloud, 'I love you.'

Chris thought that was why he always waited for Nina to say I love you first, but when she questioned him, rather than making excuses, he grabbed her face and kissed her all over, saying, "I love you. I love you. I love you." Nina knew he would do anything for her, but she deserved to hear the words.

Chris was also at his romantic peak during their trips. He dropped all talk of Black people and their struggles and White people and their lies. He didn't need to control everything and convince Nina to support him. He was more considerate of

Nina's feelings and did everything naturally to show her how appreciative and grateful he was to be her man and have her as his woman.

---

The young couple had so much fun in Florida that it was hard to leave. After three weeks, they had some more stops to make before they headed back to New York. They packed their stuff and headed to Atlanta, about six hours away. They enjoyed the drive to Atlanta, basking in the sun, the calm breeze, and the smell of palm trees.

They finally made it to the city. Chris hadn't been to visit his family there for ten years. The last time he came, it was with his father to visit his uncle, Ralph Samuel. Reverend Samuel was a pastor in Atlanta and had his own church. While the church was small, Chris remembered the people being warm and welcoming. He also remembered his father hugging his brother a lot and the two brothers leaving to go for long walks to talk. Going back to Atlanta brought back a lot of memories of his father.

Chris called his uncle, and he and his wife were waiting for the younger couple as they drove up to the house. The pastor lived in a beautiful, primarily White neighborhood in Cobb County. Chris's uncle also had another job as a hedge fund manager, and since his wife was a real estate broker, they had plenty of money. They had been married for thirty-five years and still looked happy.

When Chris and Nina pulled up, his uncle immediately grabbed the bags and led the way into the house. Chris didn't remember the house from his childhood visit. Their home was a mini-mansion with all kinds of art and antique furniture. It was gorgeous. It looked like a mini version of the castle on his college campus, with marble floors, wooden walls, and a staircase that led upwards…to heaven, it seemed. Dinner was prepared in the small dining room by the kitchen.

Their twins, Margaret — named after her mother — and Marilyn, were both over ten years older than Chris and had moved out of the house after graduating from college. Both had gone to Spelman College. Margaret was living with her husband and kids in Savannah, Georgia, and Marilyn was pursuing her Master's degree at Howard University. Uncle Ralph said Marilyn and Margaret would meet them at church on Sunday.

They wouldn't let Chris and Nina check into the hotel as they had planned but had already prepared two rooms for them. Chris would have preferred the hotel to the separation. Still, when he tried to convince his uncle that they wouldn't mind staying at the hotel, the Reverend Samuel said, "You're my favorite brother's only son, and I will not have you staying in a hotel while you are in my city. And the truth is, you aren't going to find a hotel better looking and more comfortable than my house."

*Free Nina: The College Years*

In the end, all Chris could say was, "Yes, sir."

Nina didn't mind. She loved the house and immediately felt a connection with his wife. Aunt Margaret looked at Nina, put her arms around her shoulder, and slowly led her into the living room while asking her, "So what Sorority do you belong to?" Nina was stung by the question, "What, what?" Nina asked with a squinted face.

"Oh girl, I don't know what they're teaching you all at those White schools, but it sure ain't about sisterhood. Alpha Kappa Alpha Sorority, established in 1908 on the campus of Howard University, is my choice." Nina looked at her with inquiring eyes desiring to hear more.

Aunt Margaret was just as much a Womanist as Nina. She told Nina how she had to fight the old boys club to reach her place in the real estate industry. Many of them shut her out and tried to block or steal business opportunities from her. She fought hard and, with the help of a loving and supportive husband, overcame the vultures and gained the community's respect as a businesswoman. Margaret was one of the top-selling real estate brokers in Cobb County. Her triumph enabled other women to get into the real estate profession and opened the door to other Black women in the field.

Chris had noticed that Nina sought out many Black women in their fifties and sixties to talk to. He thought that, in some ways, they made up for the loss of her mother, whom she had never gotten the chance to know. Her grandmother was loving and nurturing but unwilling to change with the times. When Nina spoke to women of Aunt Margaret's generation, she felt she could relate to them more closely. They knew how to talk to, guide, and encourage her without undermining her traditional values. Since Aunt Margaret had daughters older than Nina, she fit the bill perfectly.

While Nina and his aunt were occupied, Chris had long talks with his uncle. They spoke in his study, which was lined with wall-to-wall wooden bookshelves. There must have been hundreds of books on every subject, from law to African American Studies to business and mountain climbing. Uncle Ralph had souvenirs from around the world. He and his wife were great travelers, and Chris suspected they had been to dozens of countries and most islands.

"Wow! This is the way I want to live."

"Thanks." Uncle Ralph took Chris by his shoulders, steered him into one of the chairs, and sat across from him.

"This takes a lot of work and a lot of sacrifice, and if God desires it for you, you will have the desires of your heart. But it won't be easy."

Chris looked at him and then back at the book-lined room and thought to himself, *'For this, it would be worth the sacrifice.'*

"So, how is your mother?"

"She's fine," Chris answered.

Uncle Ralph and his mother never really got along, but he respected her and knew that his brother loved her. He didn't agree with mom for some of the same reasons Chris didn't. He also thought she should have returned to school and gotten her degree. Although Chris agreed, he felt it would be disloyal to tell his uncle. He didn't side with people against his mother.

None of Chris's father's family liked his mother's side of the family. They felt his father married down. They were an ambitious lot, successful in many areas. They worked hard, prided themselves on education, and loved the idea of excelling as Black people. On his mom's side, his family was less ambitious. His uncle was so glad when he found out that Chris had followed more in his father's footsteps. In her defense, Chris told him his mom was really into the church, which enhanced his opinion of her.

"You look more and more like your father, and your ambition holds up the banner of his life. You are your father's child."

"Thanks, uncle. My mom says the same thing."

They spoke for a long time about Chris's father. Uncle Ralph told Chris stories about when his brother was a young man and some of the stories Chris had not heard about before. Such as the tale of the time when his father was home from the military and stole a car. He was chased by the police, only to realize that the police were chasing him because he had left his wallet in the store. When they pulled him over, they gave him his wallet and told him to slow down. The police saw his military card in his wallet and assumed he was one of the good guys. After the close call, his father drove to the next town, parked the car, and walked home.

Chris knew his uncle missed his brother. The pastor kept talking about how much he meant to him. Uncle Ralph told him that a part of him died when his father died. Chris wasn't surprised when tears filled his eyes. He was feeling emotional, too.

"Your father wasn't only a brother to me. He was my best friend, someone I could trust with all that I had. I would give up all this," he waved his hand around the library, "just to have him back again."

Chris didn't know what to say. He just looked at his uncle at a loss for words. His father's death undoubtedly impacted everyone he touched in life.

His father grew up, with his brothers and sisters, in a city called Beaufort in South Carolina. They all had the same father but different mothers. Coincidentally, their mothers were sisters. Talk about scandalous. The family still didn't talk about the blood ties. Chris's dad kept his mother's last name, Raine, while Uncle Ralph took his father's last name, Samuel. Chris's dad went to New York after the war; his uncle followed a few years later. Uncle Ralph was then recruited by a firm in Atlanta and moved South and has lived there ever since. He seemed to love it. Chris asked how he got along with Southern White folks, and he snorted.

"They're a trip," he said. "But as long as they don't bother me, I don't bother them."

Uncle Ralph had been an elected city council official and retired from it about ten years ago. Retirement clearly wasn't for him. He admitted that he was thinking about getting back into politics. The problem was that the church needed his attention since it had been growing fast over the last few years. Uncle Ralph asked Chris to stay until Sunday and come to church. His nephew told him he would speak to Nina and see what she said. Ralph tapped his forehead and said, "Good move. You should always check with the missus before you make any big decisions. Your life will be much more peaceful."

Chris laughed. "I'm learning."

"Besides," his uncle joked. "They're the real bosses."

His philosophy clearly worked; his home was lovely, and his relationship with his wife and daughters was incredibly strong.

As they were talking Nina and Aunt Margaret walked into the room.

"Chris, I'm joining the Sorority," Nina stated excitedly while holding Aunt Margaret's hand. Chris's uncle looked at him and interjected, "And you need to be in a Fraternity. Alpha Phi Alpha is my choice. We'll talk about that later." Nina laughed wistfully and said, "I want to take them back home with us or stay with them."

"I don't think that will happen. We have work to do, but they will allow us to stay till Sunday because they want us to go to church," Chris told Nina. Nina knew he wasn't big on church but loved his Atlanta family. They both agreed that since they had been invited and everyone had been so kind, they should stay and go to church, then leave.

# CHAPTER TWENTY-FOUR

Sunday rolled around, and they followed in the rental car behind Uncle Ralph's big black Cadillac. They all pulled up to the church, which seemed like it was in the heart of Atlanta, and decamped from the cars. As Chris and Nina stood in the sun, Chris's cousins came forward to welcome them.

"Hey, Chris!" One of the daughters said as she embraced him. He didn't remember which sister was which, but luckily his uncle was on hand to re-introduce the cousins now that they were grown up.

"You remember Marilyn and Margaret?" He pointed at each woman to identify them as they hugged and petted him. They then turned their attention to Nina.

"Oh my God, you're so beautiful. How did you hook up with this rascal?" Margaret asked with a big laugh. They welcomed Nina with the same loving hugs they had bestowed on Chris. Nina gave them a big hug back as if she had known the women all her life.

"I hear you're going to be our Soror Sister." Marilyn and Margaret stated as they dragged Nina into the church with Chris, his uncle, and aunt in tow.

The church was a small white building with red brick ornamentation. The entrance had a big sign that read Atlanta Baptist Church. It was surrounded by a large parking lot that must have held at least fifty cars. Chris's uncle told him that the Rev. Dr. Martin Luther King Jr's former church was not far away. Chris would have liked to visit the building, but no more time was left for detours. This visit to the church was going to eat up all the extra time in their schedule.

When they entered the building, the sanctuary looked bigger than the outside of the church. It was just as gorgeous as his uncle's home. He was very tasteful and elegant in everything he touched. Chandeliers hung from the high ceiling, and a bright red carpet lay on the floor. Stained glass windows hung high on the walls on both sides of the sanctuary with murals on the glass and Jesus as a Black man. The ten rows of pews on either side of the sanctuary stretched about thirty feet back from the pulpit to the wide doors.

The choir had already begun singing from a space in the choir loft that seemed to be about 35 voices strong. The Spirit was infectious as they walked in. Nina and Chris were both filled with awe. About a hundred people were already seated in the pews, but more came in as they sat down, and Chris's uncle went to his office to prepare.

*Free Nina: The College Years*

It felt great to have family and friends surrounding them in the church. Chris had never seen Nina smile and laugh so much, and he knew it was because she felt she had a mother and sisters to whom she could relate. As glad as he was to share his family with her, Chris was equally happy that she had become part of his family.

The church choir could really sing. They were head and shoulders above the level of the choir at Quad Jam. Their harmony was spectacular. The choir didn't jump or shout, but their voices — along with the music — lifted everyone's spirit. Several members of the congregation came to their feet in praise.

The church was made up of primarily Black professionals, clearly financially well off. They were older, in their 60s and 70s, although some were the same age as Chris's cousins, Margaret and Marilyn. They had recently returned to church after leaving to wander in the world for a while. Now they were ready to settle down and raise a family, and worshipping at their father's church was a big part of their newfound maturity.

His uncle emerged from his office in his royal purple robe, and as soon as the choir finished their song, he began to speak. He introduced Nina and Chris to the congregation. Everyone applauded when their pastor told them that his niece and nephew were visiting from New York and that Chris would be starting Columbia law school in the fall. Those closest shook his hand or hugged Nina. Chris studied Nina as member after member grabbed her. He could tell she felt at home here and loved the atmosphere. The church was a contrast to her Catholic upbringing, where members in the congregation were more interactive and engaging with each other than at the Catholic church.

After the choir sang one more song, Uncle Ralph began to preach. Chris had never witnessed his uncle in his role as Pastor before, but as soon as Uncle Ralph spoke, he felt the Spirit enter him. The transformation from Uncle Ralph to Pastor Samuel was immediately witnessed by Chris. Nina, beside him, was moved, too. He could feel her intense concentration, and they shared a couple of glances, where he could tell she was impressed.

Knowing her, he understood she didn't wholly approve of Uncle Ralph's constant use of 'He' for God. She felt God was universal and should have no gender attached to God's existence. Nina also felt that if God had a gender, it would be female since all creation comes from women. They had discussed it, and he understood her objections, even if he didn't totally agree with her. But when she smiled at him and reached for his hand, he knew she felt, as he did, the constructs of gender aside, the service was moving.

For Chris, the subject matter seemed directed especially at him, as most good sermons should. Pastor Samuel spoke on the wilderness experience from the book of Exodus. "You don't know what you will have to go through in life," he intoned. "You can plan today, and something unpredictable will upset your path and plans tomorrow. God doesn't make life an easy journey. Life has all kinds of ups and downs, twists and turns. It is full of hidden grenades." Chris felt his uncle was blessing him, his current travels, and his future, establishing himself as a law student and, presumably after that, a lawyer and elected official.

Pastor Samuel spoke with passion and clarity. He used no written notes. Everything came from his head as if he had memorized every word and verse. He frequently raised his eyes to heaven. His voice boomed like Martin Luther King Jr. It was like listening to a great statesman. He was nothing like the preachers Chris had known growing up who hollered from beginning to end, jumping about and singing their hearts out, covered in sweat as if they had been caught in a rainstorm by the end of the sermon.

The weekly service at his mom's church ended with a loud crescendo that included more hollering and singing. The preachers often hurt Chris's ears with their shouting and confused him with their sermons, but Chris's uncle was clear; his baritone voice inched up and fell at different points in the sermon. He painted a vivid picture with his words so his listeners could recall their own wilderness experiences. He captured and kept Chris's attention, who listened along with the whole congregation, caught up in the suspense.

"When I was in the Army, you had to watch out for grenades because they could be planted anywhere. At any time, one could disrupt your path, disturb your life, cause death and destruction, and throw you off track. The path of life is filled with grenades that can disrupt, disturb, and throw everything out of whack." People from the congregation responded with the call of 'Amen.' Some folks spoke back, but most of them listened as if they didn't want to miss not one uttered word.

It wasn't just the message but the messenger that made Chris glad he had decided to worship at his uncle's church this Sunday morning. He related personally to what the man was preaching, and suddenly he felt a quick suspension of his breath, a feeling that held him and wouldn't loosen. The sensation reminded Chris of the deep emotion he felt when his father died and then again when his cousin was shot. He was being pulled in two different directions. His uncle's analogy felt like it was aimed directly at him as if he had actually stepped on a grenade and had been blown up into several pieces. He felt there was a tug of war going on inside of him.

It was as if his uncle could see into his soul to the moments in his life that had done so much to form him. Those traumatic moments when his life had been disrupted, pulled sharply between good and evil, life and death, wrong and right. Since then, he had constantly been trying to put his pieces back together because parts of him had been lost, stolen, blown up.

It took a huge emotional toll, and Chris couldn't help but feel emotionally broken, dismembered, and disjointed. His mind shifted as he felt suspended in time and space, his heart racing to keep pace, and his soul searching for an escape. It was like being boxed into a corner, unable to move. He wanted the bombs to stop going off and blowing up inside of him, and he wanted the men he loved to be returned to him, unhurt, and his own soul to be renewed, undamaged.

"Whatever track you find yourself on, you must know that God is with you. He will never leave nor forsake you. Though I walk through the valley of the shadow of death, I will fear no evil, for thou art with me." Chris had heard the verse before, but this time it felt real, like his uncle's sermon was leading him back through the valley of the shadow of death. Chris felt his father in his arms, his head lying there with a hole in it, the mark of the tumor that had taken his life.

Chris's cousin lay across the other arm, bleeding profusely from the stomach. Chris heard him screaming and could see the blood all over his hands. And Chris wanted to rub the blood off, but he couldn't. He tried to close off the vision, get up, and walk away, but he couldn't. He was stuck, forced to stare into the eyes of his destruction, the shadows of death and darkness, fearing evil while wanting good. He wanted out of this wilderness, this valley.

Chris focused intently on his uncle's powerful voice. "A lot of people pray to God to get them out of the wilderness, rather than pray for strength to get them through the wilderness. 'Lord, get me out of this trouble.'" Pastor Samuel's voice became more animated as he imitated the voices of the trapped calling for aid. "'Lord, get me out of this hospital.' 'Lord, get me out of this financial crisis.' I used to pray like that. When I was going through my troubles years ago, I just wanted to be out! But now, I say, 'God, give me the strength to get through this wilderness in my life.'"

"Amen!" rang out of Chris's mouth, to his surprise. He felt as if he had awakened from a deep sleep. Voices rose around him as other people in the pews related to what the pastor had said. Chris knew how they felt. It was as if he heard Chris's cries and answered his prayers. He was one of the trapped ones his uncle talked about, who wanted out because he knew he didn't have the strength to get through the pain of life alone. He heard Nina whisper Amen several times but could not look at her. He could not join her. After that involuntary Amen, Chris was speechless, but inside he was screaming, shouting, yelling to get out.

He wanted out of the nightmare, the loneliness, the wilderness. The burden of walking through the valley of the shadow of death alone. He wanted the strength to get through this, to get out of this, to let the dead bury the dead. In his soul, he was screaming, '*God give me the strength to get through this wilderness, this valley of death, of dying, of shame, of lies, of lives I held so dearly.*' He wanted his father's love, his cousin's protection, and his mother's salvation. He wanted to live his life in peace, not in pieces. He did not want to go on being at war with himself.

"If God took us out of everything without having us go through some things, how would we gain strength for our journey? If your momma got you out of all your trouble, how would you be strong enough to deal with your own problems? If daddy came running every time you made a mistake, how would you learn from your mistakes? If family members always helped you, you would give them more credit than God."

The congregation laughed but Chris cried inside as the pastor preached. "God is our refuge and strength, a very present help in the times of trouble, the Bible says. God wants us to develop the strength to get through the wilderness! The confidence to walk through the valley! The courage to confront the enemy! God wants us to endure our circumstances! God wants us to build up trust in the midst of trouble. Strength builds character, character builds faith, faith builds trust, trust builds boldness, and boldness will get you through the wilderness and into the promise of God's goodness!"

As his voice rose, so did the voices of those all-around Chris. Some stood and began to put their hands together, shaking their heads and closing their eyes as their pastor's words struck home.

Though he addressed the whole church, Chris knew that somehow, he was speaking directly to him and his situation. It was as if Pastor Samuel had a secret code to decipher his hidden pain, could reach into his thoughts and heart and trespass through his body directly to his Spirit. How did his uncle know? Who told him? What was God doing? Chris could not move. At that moment, he knew his mother couldn't save him, his father couldn't help him, and even his hero, his cousin, couldn't protect him. He would be on his own, in the valley of the shadow of death, in the wilderness of despair, in the desert of destruction. God help him!

"The children of Israel had to go through the wilderness to get to the promise." The pastor continued to preach. "When they got to the promised land, they got all the good things that came with it: a land flowing with milk and honey, a lot for themselves, and a home of their own. When you read the Bible, Joseph went from being betrayed by his brothers, falsely accused by a woman, and jailed. That was his wilderness. Remember that God has a way of turning the *wilderness into promise*. The promise is when Joseph found himself lieutenant governor of Egypt."

Cries of 'Amen!' rang out all around him, feeling to Chris as if they were right next to him and yet far away. He continued to focus on his uncle's voice. "Nelson Mandela, who was a prisoner for twenty-seven years, is now on his way to becoming the first Black president of South Africa. He went from wilderness to promise. Martin Luther King Jr. went from an unknown preacher to a national figure. He went from wilderness to promise. All of them had to go *through something* to get *to something!*" Congregants shouted. A woman, a few pews in front of Chris and Nina, stood up and began to wave her hand in the air, crying, "Amen! Yes, Lord!"

As if his uncle had turned on a tap of spiritual balm, relief swamped Chris at the word 'promise.' He finally started to feel that God would take him out of the wilderness and bring him to the promise of freedom that he had heard from his church and his mother his whole life. He finally felt he might receive the promise of salvation, protection, and peace he yearned for. The promise to let go of the past, the death, and the dying. He felt the pastor was bringing back again the promise of success and wholeness and healing and family that he felt at the beginning of the sermon. Chris was suspended at God's promise, and he felt a loosening of the chains that bound him.

"The only way to get to the promise and out of the wilderness is to hold to God's unchanging hand. Some people let go of God in the wilderness. We start complaining. We stop believing. We start thinking of ways to get out of the problem by holding onto the enemy, which can make the situation worse.

"A friend of mine was in the wilderness of no money. Has anybody ever been there?" Pastor Samuel asked the congregation. Their shouts said that they had. He continued, "He decided that after praying for so long that he would borrow some money from a friend. However, he didn't ask the friend if he could borrow it. He just took it and figured he would pay the money back when the time was right. The friend accused him of stealing the money, and he went to jail, pushing him deeper into the valley. You can't let go of God because things are not happening when you think they should! You can't take matters into your own hands because you feel like God has not answered your prayers. You have to hold to God's unchanging hand until God changes the situation."

"But this is the goodness of God: no matter where you are, you can grab God's hand, and he will pull you through." His uncle stretched out his hand and began pulling as if he were pulling someone up from the ground. "The deeper you are, the longer His arm. He will drag you through the mud, yank you out of despair, haul you out of hell, and bring you to the promise."

"Yes, he will!" one man stood and shouted. The congregation was swaying along to the rhythm of Pastor Samuel's voice, caught up in the animated delivery of his belief and captivated by the passion of his prose. Chris could feel God pulling him out of the pit through his uncle's sermon. He felt a hand on his arm, shaking him and calling his name. There was a light leading him out of darkness, and just before he climbed out of the mouth of the deep gaping hole he'd fallen into, he snapped out of his trance…to find the voice calling to him was Nina's.

"Chris, you ok?"

His head snapped in her direction, and he looked at her for a moment, trying to recollect where he was, how much time had passed and come back to reality. He smiled in relief as he found his voice, "Yes."

His voice was so loud he was sure that everyone heard him, but they were too caught up in their own jubilation. Nina didn't react as if he'd yelled, and Chris saw there were tears in her eyes as if she had gone through her own valley during the sermon.

He held her, feeling as though they both clung to each other as they did to God's unchanging hand, unwilling to let go of either.

"Don't let go, don't give up, don't stop believing. Don't allow fear, pain, hurt, loss, sickness, guilt, jail, and shame to bring you down or tear you apart. Nothing should separate you from the love of Christ! Shall trouble, or hardship, or persecution, or famine, or nakedness, or danger, or sword overcome you? No! In all these things we are more than conquerors through Christ, who loved us!" The congregation went wild at the power in Pastor Samuel's sermon. He believed every word he'd spoken, and they couldn't help but feel the strength of his conviction.

"When you get to the promise, you will be stronger, smarter, bolder, and wiser. You will shout, '*I made it! thank God, I made it!*'"

Then he began singing the old spiritual in his baritone voice:

*"I'm free!*
*Praise the Lord, I'm free*
*No longer bound*
*No more chains holding me*
*My soul is resting*
*It's just a blessing,*
*Praise the Lord, Halleluiah, I'm free."*

His Uncle dropped his head as if he were out of breath. For the moment, Chris felt free, and he loosened his hold on Nina's hand as they stood up, along with the others who weren't already on their feet, and applauded. Chris felt the Spirit of God as he had never felt it before. For him, it wasn't about church but about feeling the love of God, something he needed to get back after all these years since his father died. The anger was momentarily gone, and comfort took its place. He felt good but not complete.

The choir started singing; with arms around each other, Nina and Chris swayed with the music. Chris realized that both Nina and he could relate so well to the sermon because they had just gone through the trauma of going to jail, even if for a couple of hours. They could finally appreciate what had been necessary to achieve their goal of procuring the promise of the college to hire a Black professor. Though Chris realized it was more personal than political for both Nina and him. They both had to wrestle with their own wildernesses.

As if she knew exactly what he had been thinking, Nina shared the question that most tugged at her soul. "I wonder what it would have been like to grow up with my mom and dad," Nina whispered, wiping the tears from her eyes. All Chris could do was hold her as he wondered about the vision he had seen and the feelings he had experienced. The urge to share what had happened was strong, but he kept it to himself, not sure she would understand the darkness in the depth of his soul that, even after the cleansing relief of his uncle's sermon, he still felt looming somewhere in the distance, a threatening presence in his life.

Just then, his cousins hugged him and Nina. He didn't know if the women saw the tears in Nina's eyes or the confusion on his face, or if they were just moved to reach out to two young new family members, but it made him and Nina smile even more warmly at each other and everyone around them. The pastor called for everyone to join him in prayer for each other and asked that Nina and Chris come to the front of the line. He prayed for the young couple and a safe conclusion to their journey. He went on to pray, like a wish, that they would support each other; he prayed for them to have the strength to hold on to each other and never to let go of God's unchanging hand, no matter the circumstances.

After church, there were refreshments downstairs, and Chris and Nina got to meet some of the congregation members and linger with the family for a bit longer. Like the church folk back home, Uncle Ralph's flock of worshippers congratulated Chris for graduating from college and getting into law school, and they encouraged Nina to keep up her studies and all her good works. One man even put a hundred-dollar bill in Chris's hand. Some older women wrapped them up in maternal hugs. This was the first time that Nina and Chris together had felt a mutual connection with a church, and he told his uncle that anytime they were in town, they were definitely coming back to service again.

When it was time to leave, the whole family took turns hugging them goodbye. Chris's uncle took a moment to pull him aside while his aunt and cousins exchanged a few quiet words of farewell to Nina.

"Listen," his uncle began intensely. "I want you to stay focused on your studies. It will be hard, but you have royalty in your DNA." Chris could almost see his father in the older man's face and hear the familiar paternal tone in his voice. At that moment, it was as if his dad had returned; or God had sent someone to deliver a message from him.

"Don't allow the White law to shape you," he continued. "Instead, allow Black history to mold you and the struggle of our ancestors to guide you. Challenge the system so that you can overturn White power. Black people need Black people, and America needs Black people to continue to be its conscience. Whatever you do, don't get caught up in the corruption because it will only lead to despair."

At that moment, all Chris could say was, "Yes, Dad."

His Uncle's eyes widened in surprise, and he laughed, hugging him hard as if Chris were his son — or maybe his late brother. They spoke for a few more minutes, and he told Chris how beautiful his girlfriend was and that he should try his best to be good to her. He ordered his nephew to remain faithful and not let his penis get the best of him. Uncle Ralph told him that if he needed anything, Chris could call, and he slipped his brother's son a small wad of cash. Then they hugged one last time before the family walked the young couple to their rental car.

"Well, Nina, it was really good meeting you, and we hope to see you again. I'll send you all the information and the connection to some of our Soror sisters in New York. They'll be more than happy to have you." Aunt Margaret said as her two daughters stood on either side of Nina, each holding a hand. Nina began to tear up, and Chris smiled seeing his sentimental girlfriend bid goodbye to her newfound family.

"It was great meeting you all. I felt so wonderful and at home. I will cherish the memory of this meeting forever." Nina responded sincerely.

"Yes, Nina. Remember, we're all family, even as Womanists. We still love our men and all their issues. Hold on to God but also hold on to Chris. He's going to need you more than he knows." Aunt Margaret and her daughters surrounded Nina with a wraparound hug as Chris opened the car door for her, and he gently maneuvered her away from them and into the passenger seat.

He ran around and jumped in the driver's seat, convinced this long farewell would never end unless he took control. Chris asked Nina about her conversation with his aunt as they pulled off.

"That's between us Womanists," was the only answer she would give, and since she seemed content to leave it at that, he dropped it, figuring he would find out one day.

Before they went home, they stopped at Stone Mountain Park and climbed Stone Mountain. Stone Mountain was a beautiful historic place in Georgia. People came from all over the country to view and climb its peak. They held hands to the top of the mountain. He felt they were somehow symbolizing their commitment to each other and their determination to stay together no matter how rocky the road, difficult the days, or tumultuous the times. If he had put it into words, he would have said the gesture held a promise: they would struggle together, no matter what.

Little did they know, the wilderness was on its way.

Made in the USA
Columbia, SC
31 October 2022